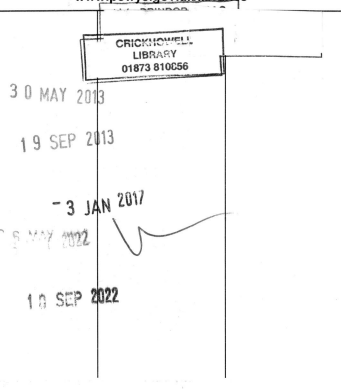
This book must be returned by the last date stamped above.
Rhaid dychwelyd y llyfr hwn erbyn y dyddiad diwethaf a stampiwyd uchod.

A charge will be made for any lost, damaged or overdue books.
Codir tâl os bydd llyfr wedi ei golli neu ei ni weidio neu heb ei ddychwelyd mewn pryd.

I dedicate this book to my sisters
Karen & Moy
with love

Kelpies is an imprint of Floris Books
First published in 2013 by Floris Books
© 2013 Janis Mackay
Janis Mackay has asserted her right under the
Copyright, Designs and Patent Act 1988 to be
identified as the Author of this work

The publisher acknowledges subsidy from
Creative Scotland towards the publication of this volume

 This book is also available
as an eBook

British Library CIP data available
ISBN 978-086315-954-1
Printed in Poland

1

It was Saturday, 15th December, 2012, and it was quarter to ten in the morning. I know it sounds weird to be so exact about it, but this story's got a lot to do with time. That was when Mum sent me along to the corner shop to buy her newspaper, a packet of Jaffa Cakes and something for myself costing no more than 30p. She called it A Mission of Trust. Thing is, I'd been grounded three times that month for sneaking out when I was supposed to be in my room doing homework. But for three days I had behaved, meaning I'd stayed in. With the doors and windows locked I didn't have much choice.

I have a den and that's where I usually hung out when I wasn't grounded, but Mum didn't know about the den. Nobody knew about it, except Will and Robbie who are in my gang. The den is a shed no one uses now in a big, old abandoned garden, and it's our gang hut. It's the best and I'll tell you more about it but, like I said, for three days I stayed away, lounging about in my room, dreaming about the seriously cool bike I wanted for Christmas.

When Mum popped her head round the door, carrying a twin on each hip, and said, "Right, Saul, I'm letting you go round to the shop," I could feel this major whine coming on. Like I *really wanted* to go round to the shop. I didn't. I was cosy, sprawled out on my blue beanbag seat and leafing through my BMX magazines, circling the bike I wanted and the helmet and stickers and stuff. Plus it was cold outside – in fact the man on the telly said there was a good chance of snow that night. A trip to the den, maybe. Getting stuff for Mum at the shop, no thanks. The twins started crying and pulling at Mum's hair. "I'm trusting you, Saul," she said, yanking her hair back. "And you've to come straight home." I was ready to moan till I remembered Christmas was just ten days away. I thought about the BMX and all the extras I wanted and decided I needed to look good right now. I jumped up, fell back, then struggled out of my beanbag and chirped, "Yeah, ok Mum."

Mum parked the twins on my bed, sighing like it was all too much for her. Boy, could they howl! She shoved my old hat down over my ears and handed me the exact money, because occasionally I've helped myself to some spare change. "Thirty pence for you," she said. I could feel another moan coming on but held it in. You might as well chuck 30p in the river and make a wish. A Milky Way's about all you can buy with 30p, and that's over in two bites. Then I thought maybe I *would* chuck my 30p in the river and wish for a BMX, because with my parents and their lack of money – specially now I had two baby sisters, who "need clothes and food and prams and nappies galore," I couldn't be too sure all the presents on my list would show up, no matter how chirpy I was. Never mind the bike; I wasn't sure I'd get anything on my list! Mum picked up the twins and steered me out of my room, along the hallway and out the front door. "Remember Saul," she shouted so the whole street could hear, "I'm trusting you."

Once I'd got going, it felt great to be out on my own. I slowed down, wanting this freedom to last. I was already spinning stories to tell mum when I got back – how there was a huge queue in the shop and I had to wait aaaaages! And how the ice made me walk really slow. The sky looked dark and heavy, like it might snow. The few folks I met along the street thought so too.

"Hi Saul. Good to see you. With a bit of luck we'll have a white Christmas, eh?"

"Hey Saul, not seen you about for a wee while. It's going to snow. I swear it is. You can build a snowman."

I am well known in the street cause I always say hi to everybody. Except Crow, the town bully and the one person in the world I was scared of. Like, really scared. His real name is Colin Rowe, but everybody calls him Crow. Even his name is scary. Crow is in second year, and he's seriously hard. If I spotted him, I crossed the street or backtracked into the house. But Crow wasn't prowling around that Saturday morning, 15th December. Crow probably hated getting cold. Crow hated lots of things – including me. But I didn't want to spoil this little freedom trip thinking about him too much.

I liked looking at Christmas trees in people's windows, especially ones with flashing lights, so I hung about doing that for a while. I counted nine of them, but as I wandered past the laundrette, I was itching to nip up the lane behind it, bolt along the cuddy, clamber over the wall, race across the overgrown wasteland, wriggle through the gap in the hedge and zip into my den. Some other gang might have claimed it while I'd been stuck in at home. Crow might have wrecked it!

My gang reckons once upon a time the den was somebody's garden shed. It leans over to the side a bit, so Robbie (who has been to Italy) called it Pisa after some leaning tower there. The den is at the edge of a rambling wild garden with some ancient trees in it. There must have been a fantastic big house there. Officially the garden's in a demolition site, surrounded by a barbed wire fence then a thick hedge. It's full of nettles and rubbish and gangly old rhubarb stalks and dead birds. As well as the fence, there's a sign saying,

DEMOLITION SITE
DANGER OF DEATH
KEEP OUT

And in case you can't read, there's a scary skull and crossbones next to it. But you can get in through a gap in the hedge round the back where the barbed wire is slack. Only me, Will and Robbie knew about that.

The den is on the edge of town and Robbie said it was like time forgot about it, which was kind of funny considering what happened. The den was a bit creepy when we first found it, but we flicked away the cobwebs, kicked out the two dead mice and the dead rabbit, then put nice things inside to make it cosy.

Will brought his old cuddly ewok toy from when he was younger. It's called Fred and is the den mascot. He guards the place when nobody's there. Robbie brought a few old chipped ornaments, like a china dog, a blue plastic bowl (for crisps, he said) and a photo of him when he was seven, grinning in a fancy frame. I brought along a stripy blanket and a cushion and some pens to write our names on the wall. There was a wooden box in the shed filled with old gardening magazines, and we hauled in stones and bits of wood to make wee benches. It looked brilliant.

Anyway, there I was, wandering up the street towards the shop and dreaming about the den. I could see on the church clock that it was five to ten. I was walking so slow I was practically going backwards. I tried to stop dreaming about the den. The thing was, I told Will and Robbie that the gang would have a break for a bit, cause last time we were there, last weekend, it was perishing cold. Will and I were being crims on the run from the police and Robbie was being the policeman who was trying to arrest us, and we were trying to blackmail him with a few thousand quid we had stashed away in the gardening magazines and the game was really good and it was mostly my idea, but suddenly Robbie said he was freezing and he wanted to go home. Then Will piped up and said, actually, he was freezing too. So I said, "Right, fine, we'll take a break till the weather gets better."

We all looked about and were silent for a moment till Robbie said, "Pisa is like our other home, isn't it?"

Me and Will nodded. It was.

It was now one minute to ten. The corner shop came into view. I felt something wet brush my cheek. I looked up. White flecks were swirling through the air and landing on me. I like snow. I opened my mouth to catch a snowflake. One landed on my tongue, which was exactly when the church bells rang for ten o'clock, which was exactly when a car screeched its tyres, blared its horn and someone screamed really loudly.

I swung round to see a screaming girl in fancy dress standing stock-still in the middle of the road, her arms flung out to the side and her face pale as a ghost. The screeching car swerved round her, and roared off. Her screams turned to whimpers and gasps. She stumbled across the road in a panic, tripped over the kerb and fell at my feet. She buried her face in her hands and started sobbing.

I looked around for her mum or big sister or someone, but no one was there. So I bent down and patted her on the shoulder, feeling seriously awkward. "Hey," I said, "are you ok?"

She pulled her hands away from her face, stopped crying and gazed up at me, like I was some kind of superstar. I got the weirdest feeling, like a million hot needles jabbing up my spine. I'd never seen anyone like her. She had pale blue eyes, totally white, practically see-through skin, a funny shower-cap-style hat on, with long twisty red hair spilling out from it and reaching all the way down her back. She stretched her hands out, then wrapped her long fingers around my ankles.

"I have become lost," she sobbed.

2

I felt trapped. The weird girl didn't let go of my ankles.
A shiver shot up my legs. I laughed, I couldn't help it.
Sometimes I laugh when I'm nervous. Then I tried
to wriggle free but this girl was seriously strong. She
clung on, like she was drowning and I was a lifeguard.
So I tried talking. "Hey, are you on your way to a fancy
dress party?" Though it was kind of early in the day
for a party. She stared up at me, all baffled, like I was
talking Chinese. "Christmas party maybe?" I went on,
smiling down at her awkwardly. But all she did was
stare, wide-eyed and terrified looking. She still had her
long fingers locked around my ankles. My heart raced.
What if she was mad? "Oh, well," I chirped, "never
mind about parties." I tried to sound chilled but inside
my panic level was rising fast. "Right then, I better get
going." Except I couldn't move. So I tried smiling to
make her relax. "Good that you're ok. Umm, see you
then. And you better look where you're going next time
you cross the road." It felt like she was going to let me
go, but at that moment another car drove past. She
shrieked and gripped my ankles even tighter. "Hey!
Excuse me!" I shouted at her. I was getting pretty
freaked out. "Could you let me go?"

She must have understood because she loosened her grip. I nodded and showed her my open hands like they do in films. It worked: she let go. "Thanks," I said, though it felt like a dumb thing to say. She should have said sorry. I took a step back, pretty fast. My ankles throbbed. She sat up and wiped her tears with her sleeve.

That's when I really saw her clothes. She wore a long brown dress with a ruffled collar and frilly bits around the sleeves. Over the brown dress she had on another sleeveless dress that was cream coloured. She looked totally old fashioned. Even her face with her lips like a doll's and her upturned nose seemed old fashioned. "Party?" she said, sitting on the pavement and gazing up at me, jittery and confused, like she had just come out of a nightmare. She twisted her long hair round her fingers and I could see tears welling up in her eyes. "Forgive me but I dinna understand."

She's got something wrong with her, I thought, taking another step back. I wondered if I should run and get a grown up? Everything about her was weird and her voice had the funniest accent I ever heard. The next second I thought, it's a joke – I'll be on YouTube with the title "Pranked!" Maybe Crow had set this up? I glanced round but nobody was on the street. There were no cameras. Nothing. The snow was falling seriously now. Part of me thought I should just get on to the shop and leave this funny girl kneeling on the pavement for somebody else to deal with but she gazed up at me with such helpless eyes. It was too awkward to walk on and just leave her. She didn't seem to know where to go. "Where. Do. You. Live?" I spoke slowly in case she was foreign or didn't understand things very well. "Live?" I repeated, louder, "*Where do you live?*"

She pointed to the corner shop. "There," she said.

I wondered if Mr and Mrs Singh had adopted a girl. "Right," I went on, "do you want me to take you into the shop, I mean, into your house?"

She nodded. Then she clutched at my hoodie and hoisted herself up to her feet. She gasped and wobbled for a moment like she was going to keel over. I felt her hands hold my arms. She was skinny but I couldn't believe how strong she was. "I'm Saul and I'm twelve," I lied.

"My name is Miss Agatha Black," she said. She took a deep breath then slowly let go of my arms. Next thing she held out a trembling hand for me to shake. "And I am eleven years and six months old."

Same as me! I shook her hand, which was very slim and cold. I felt a bit foolish shaking hands. I mean, it's not something I do. I had shaken hands three times before but always with adults, never with someone my own age. She curtsied slightly, then it dawned on me: she must be an actress. I laughed out loud, half relieved, half embarrassed. "Are you in a film?"

"A film of snow and confusion," she replied lifting her hand to catch a snowflake. I thought that was a weird title for a film, but everything about this girl was weird. I was going to say more about films when she started crying again. Pointing to the shop she sobbed, "It was here. Aye, I am utterly convinced. This time he has made a grand blunder. My life. My home. It has all gone." She wrung her pale hands together and looked totally miserable. "I was to look about me and take note, but for a moment," she said, as though I knew what she was on about. "A moment – that was all."

I needed things to get back to normal. "So, like, haha, what's the joke, Agatha?"

"This isna a laughing matter, Saul." She took my hand again and squeezed it tight. "Believe me, I am exceedingly lost and wish sorely to return home directly. The great noise shocked me straight to the core. I was to gaze about me, note the changes then hasten back." By this time she was pulling at her hair, in a right state. Then I saw her look at the ground like she had lost something. Next thing she was staring at the road. She stepped off the kerb and was about to run in front of another car. I pulled her back, just in time. "Hark! The rumbling carriage!" she squealed. "But the morsel of gold lies buried hereabouts," she cried, all flustered, not realising I'd just saved her life. I saw the driver shake his fist at us, then he was gone. The girl swung round and clasped my hands in hers. "Please," she begged, "help me find my way?"

I laughed nervously. "Well to start with, stay off the road, ok? Jeez, you gave me a fright." She nodded, squeezed my hands then stared again at Mrs Singh's shop. I took a deep breath. "I thought you said this was your home – right here?"

She was creeping me out, but I didn't mind her holding my hand.

She shook her head. "It is and it isna. It *was* my home. Oh mercy, I need to return back, Saul. It was to be but a brief journey. I imagine yea canna understand. I have to hasten back! And the gold is quite lost."

Everything was turning quiet, the way it does with

snow. "Back?" I repeated, feeling that shiver up my neck again.

She gazed at me with her pale eyes, nodded her head then said in a low voice, "Aye, Saul, back to 1812."

I couldn't help laughing, but it came out kinda squeaky. "He-he-he!" I stared at her. She wasn't laughing. "So, Agatha, you're kidding me, right?" She shook her head so her long hair swung. Snowflakes landed on her eyelashes. My heart was beating hard. She kept hold of my hand but said nothing. "You're s..s..serious?" I stammered.

She nodded.

I gulped. "How... how come?"

She sighed. "Ach Saul, tis an awfa long story." Lowering her voice to a whisper she said, "Yea see, Saul, I am the dutiful daughter of Mister Albert Black."

She stared at me like she was waiting for something. For me to nod my head, laugh and say, "Oh, right, *the* Albert Black? Him?" But I didn't say a word. When it was obvious the name Albert Black meant nothing to me, she cast her eyes down and wrung her small hands together. "He," she continued, "is a time traveller – or I should say, an ill-starred apprentice, eager to master the hidden art of travelling through time. And I, his sole child, am his assistant!"

I nodded, as though I understood, which of course I didn't. Maybe I was still on my beanbag, dreaming? But I wasn't. We were standing on the pavement, in the snow. This was real. Agatha sighed again. "So now Saul, perhaps yea comprehend my predicament? 'Tis an awfy pickle."

Miss Agatha Black knew some big words. She talked like an old granny, not a child. She rolled her Rs like a motorbike revving over cobbles. Prrrrrrrrredicament. And what the heck was predicament anyway? "The fact that yea havna heard of Mister Albert Black puts me in the doldrums, Saul," she said. "It tells me he failed. He was ever thus, born under a halfpenny planet. He didna succeed to shine out in the great books of history as he so desired. He has much to learn regarding the secret art of time travel and, what's more, he has left me here – an experiment gone horribly wrong, lost in the future."

And we were left standing in the falling snow outside the shop, me and this strange girl, who had just told me, with her hand on her heart, that she came from two hundred years ago. The snow fell faster and thick flakes swirled around us. I felt a bit embarrassed with her staring helplessly into my eyes, but in a strange way I was excited too, like I'd just landed in a real adventure. Mad as it sounded, and I wasn't ruling out the possibility that Agatha was totally off the rails, part of me believed her – or wanted to. She seriously sounded old fashioned. She looked the part and didn't seem to have a clue about the Highway Code. I had to get Mum's newspaper and Jaffa Cakes, but bumping into a girl from another time was definitely the most interesting thing that had ever happened to me, and I decided to play along with Agatha's story.

"Wanna see what your house is like now?" I suggested, trying to sound breezy. She nodded, slipped her hand under my elbow and in we went.

3

Mrs Singh looked up from the cash register, waved at me and winked. It was an "I like your new girlfriend" wink. I shook my head hard, meaning, "no – it isn't what you think."

"Hi, Mrs Singh, this is Agatha," I blurted out, guiding her up towards the counter. Then out popped lie number two, "and she's making a history film."

"Well now, isn't that a marvellous thing," Mrs Singh said, looking her up and down. "Your costume is very realistic, dear."

Agatha's jaw fell seeing Mrs Singh and her lovely red sparkly sari. If Agatha really was from 1812, then maybe she'd never seen someone from India before? Mrs Singh just smiled at Agatha then busied herself fishing for the Saturday newspaper, without me having to ask for it. "I am very fond of history myself," she went on. "Scotland is steeped in history. That's what we like about this town. You know this shop was built in 1770? History is very present for us in Peebles, don't you agree, Saul?"

I nodded, though truth was I'd never thought about it before – apart from the fact the den was obviously a pretty old garden shed.

Agatha slipped away from my arm and wandered

around the shop. I watched her gaping at the rows of brightly coloured magazines and the shelves of biscuits and the tins and light bulbs. She reached out to touch them, trembling as if a tin of soup might leap off the shelf and bite her.

"Is my shop going to be in the film?" Mrs Singh asked, leaning over the counter and lowering her voice, "because if so, I'd like some warning." She flashed her big beaming smile. "You know – to put on a touch of lipstick!"

I shrugged my shoulders and laughed, the way I did when I was feeling nervous, then quickly took a packet of Jaffa Cakes and a Milky Way from the shelf. The Milky Way was 29p. I still could, I thought, throw 1p in the Tweed and make my Christmas wish. The river wouldn't know the difference. Mrs Singh took the money, whispering as she put the things into a bag, "Has the actress never seen a shop before?" Just at that moment, Agatha appeared by my side, her face all flushed and her bottom lip trembling like she might cry. She ran her fingers over the plastic counter, winced, then pulled back, looking seriously confused. Next thing she started gaping at a box of oranges like she couldn't believe what she was seeing. With a shaking hand she reached out and stroked the dimpled orange peel. Then she bent forward and sniffed it.

"She's getting into the part," I replied hurriedly, thinking it was high time me and Agatha Black made a rapid exit.

"So I can see. But, film or not, the lassie needs a coat. It's snowing outside." Mrs Singh was a kind woman and though she loved Scotland's history she wasn't a great fan of its weather. She hurried into the back shop and was out again in half a minute with an old coat. "Someone left this here," she explained. "They never did come back to find it, so here you are, Agatha, put that on. It's a bit big, but it'll keep you warm."

"Thanking yea kindly," Agatha said.

Mrs Singh looked perplexed, then her face broke into a smile. She bowed her head and replied, "Yea are most welcome."

I took Agatha and her coat and propelled her out of the shop, calling, "Bye Mrs Singh," over my shoulder. Agatha, I thought, could be a major embarrassment.

Out on the snowy pavement she struggled into the big brown coat. The bottom of it trailed along the ground making her look like a child tramp. We hurried along the street, with Agatha nearly tripping as she gazed around – at the houses, the road, the parked cars, the television aerials, the street lamps. Sometimes she lifted her hand to catch a snowflake.

My mind was in a whirr. No way could I bring this nutty girl home. Mum would go all health-and-safety and poor Agatha would be carted off to some children's home. Then she'd never get back to 1812. No. I found her. She asked *me* to help her. I took a deep breath and smiled at poor bewildered Agatha, who flashed me such a sunny smile back that I decided there and then I *would* help her.

Den, I thought. "Come on Agatha," I said, steering her up past the launderette. Huge washing machines chugged away inside, steaming up the windows. Agatha pressed her nose up against the glass and stared, until I pulled at the sleeve of her baggy coat. "We've got to hurry," I said urgently. "Come on. Trust me; the launderette's no big deal."

Agatha, looking totally gob-smacked, didn't agree. But she followed me up the lane. I felt excited. Something big was happening. I didn't know what, but my heart was racing. We ran over the snowy slippery cobbles. Despite her little black lace up boots, long dress, shower cap hat and now long baggy coat, this Agatha Black was a fast runner. We slithered on the cobbles, climbed the wall and ran over the wasteland which was now white with snow. And all the time I could see Agatha, wide-eyed, gazing around her. She's taking notes, I thought, so she can tell her dad what she sees.

We reached the hedge, found the secret gap and wriggled through. Me being the gang leader, of course I went first. I told Agatha to hang on to my scarf and follow me. My heart leapt seeing the den again. Apart from the snow on the squint roof, it was just like we'd left it. Crow hadn't been there – phew!

"Welcome to Pisa," I said, sweeping my arm theatrically towards it. "Ta-da!" The den looked cool dusted with snow. The snow had covered all the rubbish in the garden too, which made it look magical instead of abandoned. It was the garden Agatha was staring at: the big trees, the expanse with extra fencing where a big old house must once have stood. I felt a bit miffed that she hardly noticed the den. I pushed open the shed door, which creaked like it always did. "Wanna come in?" I called, but Agatha was too busy gaping. She'd fallen all silent. Slowly she turned towards me and I saw a tear glisten on her cheek.

"Pray, where has Grandfather's house gone? The yew tree still stands, but where, alas… is his house?"

"Hey, Agatha," I said, tugging the sleeve of her coat gently, "two hundred years is, like, a long time. Houses fall down."

If it was possible for her pale face to turn any paler, it did. "What did yea say?"

"I said: houses fall down."

"No, no, – about the time."

"I said two hundred years is a long time."

I watched her working out the maths on her fingers. She looked ready to burst into tears so I jumped to the rescue, trying to sound all confident. "Hey, Agatha, no worries. If you got here, you'll get back. Come on in, I want to show you our den."

She gasped. "Two hundred years." She shook her head, she wrung her hands, she said it again, and again, "two hundred years… so much time."

Which reminded me of my own problems. It was almost half-past ten. I'd been gone ages. Mum would ground me again. Looking stunned, Agatha drifted into the den and sank down on a stone. "Two hundred years," she repeated, shaking her head. "So Father succeeded? I thought he was boasting. When he said I would travel far I dared to imagine twenty, perhaps thirty years." She shuddered. Her breath came in little rasps till I thought she might faint. I fumbled in my pocket and handed her the Milky Way. In the distance I heard the church clock chime the half hour.

"Look, Agatha," I said, "I'm really sorry but I have to go. I'll come back. But, you'll be fine here. This is my secret den. Only me and Will and Robbie know about this place. We're a gang. Do you know what that is?"

Agatha shook her head. Her long hair loosened flakes of snow down onto the wooden floor of the den. "Well, I'm the leader of it," I went on, "and we do stuff. You know? Games and stuff. Adventures. Anyway, don't wander off anywhere, ok? I'll be back as soon as I can. And – I'll bring you some food."

Agatha gazed at the Milky Way as though she didn't know what it was. "Hey, you can eat this," I said, pulling the wrapper off for her. "See." I demonstrated. "You bite into it."

She nibbled a morsel, screwing up her face like it was poison. But it seemed to help her forget about two hundred years. "How exceedingly strange," she said, nibbling like a rabbit, "and remarkably sweet." Her eyebrows arched. She shuddered, but went on nibbling, politely. I wondered when chocolate bars had been invented? Agatha had been through enough. I didn't want to kill her with a Milky Way. So I snatched back what was left of the bar and shoved it in my mouth. I picked up Fred. "Here," I mumbled, my mouth full, "have the ewok instead. He'll look after you." She squealed with delight and clasped Fred to her. I felt sorry for her, sitting there on a stone with a baggy brown coat on and hugging Will's ragged old ewok, looking like her heart might break.

"So, Agatha," I said, stepping backwards to the door. "What kind of food do you like?"

"Apples," she replied, "and roasted chestnuts. Pigeon pie and frumenty. Not gooseberries, for they do make my teeth water, but, oh – and if there is a confectionary to be had, I'd be awfa grateful."

"Right then," I said, wishing I'd never asked. "I'll see what I can do. Um, see you soon."

"At what time exactly?" she asked.

Agatha Black, I guessed, cared a lot about time. Me, I hadn't usually bothered much about it. I usually slept in and was often late for school. My mind raced. I reckoned with a bit of luck I could manage to sneak out again after lunch. "When you hear the church bells chime two o'clock, I'll be back," I said confidently, hoping somehow I'd manage.

"Ah! The kirk still stands then." She sounded relieved. "Unlike poor Grandfather's great house." She smiled, like she was making an effort to be cheery. "I look forward to our meeting," she said, pulling a little white hankie from her frilly sleeve. "Until then, dear Saul, I am much indebted to you." And she waved her wee hankie up and down, like I was royalty.

"That's ok," I said then grinned and added, mimicking her accent, "until then, dear Agatha."

I was shooting out the door of the den when she called after me. "Begging your pardon Saul, but afore yea hasten away can yea tell me – is this the year two thousand and twelve?"

I grinned and stuck my thumb up. "You got it Agatha, it is, for a few more days."

She shook her head and hugged Fred even tighter. As I headed off to the hedge I heard her mutter, "he did it. Upon my honour, Father actually did it! I am in the future!"

4

I ran all the way home, slipping on the snowy pavements.

"Just as well for you, son," Mum said, as soon as I fell into the hallway, shaking snow off my hoodie and holding up a wet newspaper and a soggy packet of Jaffa Cakes like trophies. She smiled, happy to see the Jaffa Cakes in one piece. "I was just wondering where you'd got to. I suppose you couldn't resist flinging a snowball or two, hmm?" I nodded and handed over the goods. "Well," she went on, "I was going to give you two more minutes." She laid the newspaper and the Jaffa Cakes on the top of the radiator, put on her angry face and said, "Aye, then I would have been sending Santa a message, telling him to drop something down the chimney for the twins, but give their big brother a miss this year. Well, I'm glad it turns out I could trust you after all."

I laughed; of course I don't really believe in Santa but it doesn't hurt for Mum to think I do! I flashed Mum my charming smile. If I could just keep up this good behaviour for ten more days I would surely get *something*. I wanted a bike so bad. Robbie had one. Will had one. Everyone except me. And I didn't just want any old bike – I wanted a BMX, the best BMX. "I'll be good, Mum," I cooed, but at the same time thinking how the dramatic arrival of Miss Agatha Black could seriously mess up my Christmas-present behaviour plan. Sneaking off to feed her in the den was going to make things tricky.

"Thought I'd give my room a clean," I chirped, still smiling. My cheeks were beginning to ache.

"Ah ha," mumbled Mum, tucking into a limp Jaffa Cake, "glad Santa's having an impact." Still smiling I reached out to help myself to a Jaffa Cake. She grabbed my hand. "Ask nicely," she said. "And don't forget, Santa's got the twins to see to this year. You're not the only one anymore, so don't expect big things."

As if I could forget the twins. On cue one of them started bawling. Mum dashed off to their room, leaving me free to wolf down several Jaffa Cakes, wondering how on earth I was going to get hold of the kind of food Agatha fancied. There were some apples in the fruit bowl. And there was a stall on the High Street where a man sold roasted chestnuts. I didn't have a clue what confectionary meant. And I only had 1p left.

I went off to my room and made a start at stacking all my magazines. I could earn some credit here with Mum. I watered my neglected cactus, which looked desert dry, if not dead. I arranged my school books and shoved a pile of clothes under the bed. Much neater. I emptied the contents of my rucksack onto the bed. A couple of mouldy half-eaten egg sandwiches tumbled out. They smelt gross. I could hardly palm them off on Agatha.

Underneath them was my history jotter and – wham! – I had a brilliant idea. Somewhere I had an entry form for the Scottish Borders Young Historian of the Year award. The first prize, for, "the most imaginative and realistic writing about life in times past," was £200. Ok, I had read enough bike magazines to know top of the range BMXs cost way more than that, but maybe £200 would buy a pretty good one? If I had £200, I wouldn't be depending on Mum and Dad getting the bike for me; if Christmas goes wrong, I could sort it out for myself. And maybe, just maybe, I could win it! Usually I never bothered with these competitions. There were too many swots who usually won. But those swots didn't have a real life example of Scottish history in their den. Excited, I rummaged around in my bag and eventually found the entry form scrunched up down the bottom. I threw myself down on the beanbag, smoothed out the paper and read the rules:

– Entrants must be 12 or under and living in the Borders.
– Your essay can be about any period of Scottish history before 1980.
– Your essay must be at least 500 words long – AND MUST BE YOUR OWN WORK. Handwritten or typed essays are acceptable.
– Entries are due in by 19th December. Prize-winners will be announced on 21st December.

Good luck!

I stared at the entry form. I could feel my pulse quicken. I could win this competition. For the first time in my life I really thought I could win something. Carefully I slid the form back in my schoolbag. I could hear Mum hoovering in the living room. The twins were sleeping. I glanced out the bedroom window. It was still snowing. I sank into my comfy beanbag chair and thought about what I could do with £200.

Bikes cycled around in my head. They did fabulous jumps. They twirled in the air. If I had £200 I could surely get a bike. I wouldn't have to depend on my completely unreliable parents. Or Santa.

When Mum called me for lunch I dashed into the kitchen, not wanting to be late like normal. She looked round at me, amazed. "Baked potatoes and cheese," she announced, carrying them over to the kitchen table. "Being grounded for three days obviously did the trick. Just wait till Dad gets home. I'll tell him he has a brand new responsible son."

My dad is called Rory. He's a taxi driver and weekends are when he makes his money. That's good for him but kind of bad for me because it means we don't get to hang out together much. But I guess at least he's never gone and lost me in the future. I bit into the hot potato and imagined what it would be like if I suddenly got catapulted into 2212. Seriously scary. I don't think I'd cope with it. I'd be the only human in a zombie world. Or I'd be the only one who couldn't fly or mind-read or something.

"What's 'apprentice' mean," I asked, mouth full as per usual.

"Swallow what's in your mouth, then you can ask me."

So I did. Mum said, "People who learn things. Mostly a trade, like someone who's learning to be a joiner or a painter and decorator."

"Or a taxi driver?"

Mum made a funny wee snort. "No. There's nothing to driving a taxi. I could do it. And with Sat Navs, they don't even have to know their way about like they used to."

"Yeah, but you have to know how to drive well." I stuck up for my dad. I was quite often sticking up for Dad. See, I reckoned Mum was a bit disappointed with Dad being a taxi driver and not earning much money. Her best friend's husband was an engineer, whatever that meant. The way Mum said "engineer" you'd think it meant First Minister.

"Yes, that's right," Mum said, "your dad is a good driver. We'll give him that. Anyway, you're a bit young to be thinking about apprenticeships." She ruffled my hair, sighed and said, "Enjoy being young, Son." Then she got on with feeding the twins. Soon as her back was turned I slid what was left of my baked potato off my plate and into my pocket. I knew potato wasn't exactly pigeon pie but reckoned it was similar, probably better. It was nearly half past one. As I was no longer officially grounded, I took a risk.

"Will and Robbie'll be down at the sledging hill. It'll be the best fun ever. I love the snow. I love it more than sun."

Mum narrowed her eyes and gave me the look.

"I'll be back by three," I added quickly, bouncing up

from the table. I felt the potato squishy in my pocket. "Oh, and I better have some fruit; five a day and all that." Everything was going really well, so I thought I'd risk my luck. "Oh yeah, and, um, do we have any of that confectionary stuff left?"

Mum, eyeing me strangely, chewed on a bit of potato skin while feeding Esme and making coo-coo noises to Ellie. Ellie was banging her fist on the table of her high chair. "The what stuff? I can't hear you."

I waved my hand through the air like I was swatting a fly. "Never mind." I headed for the door.

"You can wash these dishes first," Mum said, raising her voice above Ellie's din. I stepped backwards, clasping my hand over my bulging pocket and doing a funny side-step dance to the sink.

"As it happens," Mum said, "I need to buy a few things in town and the girls always sleep better after they've had fresh air." She whisked the twins out of their high chairs and left me to clear up. "Three o'clock," she called from the hallway, "means…"

I finished her sentence for her, the way she wanted me to. "Three o'clock!"

Then off she went. I couldn't believe my luck. I splashed about with the dishes, then took the squished-up potato from my pocket and stuffed it, plus a pork pie that I found in the fridge, into a plastic bag. I reckoned that pork pie was old fashioned enough. Then I grabbed three apples, a banana, a packet of crisps and a packet of marshmallows. Then I saw that word written on the back of the packet – confectionary! I felt like a detective, working things out. "Just you wait,

Agatha Black from 1812," I said out loud, throwing the blue-and-pink bag in the air. "Saul Martin is bringing you confectionary!" Then I found a can of Irn-Bru and flung that in. I fished out my sleeping bag and a pillow.

I was ready to go, except it was awkward carrying a pillow, so I stuffed it up the front of my hoodie like I was really fat. Snickering to myself I sneaked off out the back door and took the back lane so no one would see me.

Next to the pillow my heart was racing. I felt like I was heading off on a serious adventure. All the adventures I had had with Will and Robbie were just made-up ones – for the first time in my life, this was real.

5

I didn't usually take the back lane in case I bumped into Crow, but it was snowing and I took the risk. It would save time, and Crow, I was pretty sure, wasn't the type to go out in the snow. Just my luck I was wrong. First thing I smelt was the pongy cigarette smoke. Then I saw a curl of blue smoke. Next I saw this dark shape huddled in a doorway. My heart thumped. I lowered my head and kept going. The lane was narrow and I was going to have to walk right past. Maybe he wouldn't recognise me, all pillow-fat like I was. I got closer, then I heard him spit. The spit landed right in front of my feet.

"Where ya goin', fat boy?" He made a horrible sneering noise. I was so scared I was shaking, but things suddenly went my way. Behind me, I heard the laundrette door open with a squeak, and Hallelujah! – there was Crow's mum belting up the lane and swearing at him about smoking. She looked ready to cuff him one, but he snuck off.

So did I, the opposite way. I ran up the lane and pulled myself over the wall. With every step I tried to forget about Crow. I thought about Agatha Black, and her dad, and time travel, and confectionary instead.

By the time I reached the wasteland I was panting like I'd run a marathon. I was about halfway over it when I smelt burning. Maybe Crow had been here and set the den on fire? Maybe he had killed Agatha? I upped the pace, slipping on the snow. I could see a wisp of smoke curling into the air. I squirmed through the gap in the hedge and when I came out the other side breathed a sigh of relief. Pisa was still leaning. In the middle of the garden a little bonfire was burning. And from somewhere nearby I could hear Agatha laughing, but I couldn't see her. I dashed towards the bonfire. "Agatha?" I called out. "Where are you?"

"Hello. I am making angels," she called. I swung round to see Agatha lying in the snow whipping her arms up and down. She laughed again then jumped up and ran to me. "Oh Saul! Is it not a marvel?" She pointed down to the shape she'd made in the snow. It was.

"Nice one," I said. "You've made yourself some company."

She laughed again and brushed the snow off, then flopped down on the fallen log. That log, I knew for a fact, used to be over near the fence. I stared at Agatha in amazement. She must have dragged it. "Come and warm yourself by the fire," she said, patting the log for me to sit down. She was sitting on Mrs Singh's big coat. She pulled it from under her and draped it over her shoulders. "Ah! Warm as toast," she murmured.

I gazed about, seeing the garden all afresh. The scene was like a Christmas card, with the white snow and the glowing red flames and behind it the evergreen tree. "Well, I'm back," I said, "and I brought you some survival stuff." I swung my rucksack down in front of me, but I couldn't help gaping at her crackling log fire. The sticks were all arranged in spires exactly like the way it shows you to make fire in *The Dangerous Book for Boys*.

She smiled at me. "I am glad indeed to see yea, Saul. I missed yea." That was the first time anyone said that to me.

I whistled and looked into the crackling fire. "Cool fire, by the way," I said. "How did you do it?"

"It isna cool I hope. 'Tis hot."

I laughed. "I mean – it's good. I'm impressed."

"I have had a great deal of practice," she answered, deftly slinging a twig into the flames. "I was obliged to use one of your coloured books to catch the spark from the stones. I am sorry, Saul."

"No probs," I said, amazed. Agatha Black had actually started the fire without matches. In my mind I started my prize-winning essay.

In 1812 girls made fires. They rubbed stones together to catch sparks.

I grinned, imagining the head teacher calling out my name at the special prize ceremony. "Saul Martin – first prize!"

"It is actually not difficult," Agatha said, cutting in on my daydream.

"Sure," I muttered, as if I started fires by rubbing stones together all the time. It felt warm on my face. I half-expected to see a skinned rabbit roasting on a spit, but could tell by Agatha's clothes and voice that she wasn't like an orphan or beggar, like you see in films. She seemed more of a lady and ladies probably didn't go around skinning rabbits. But, posh or not, Agatha could make fire, which was more than me, Will or Robbie could. We'd had our gang a whole year and never once made a fire. Loads of pretend ones. Loads of pretend everything. But never real.

The church bells rang out for two o'clock. "Two after noon," announced Agatha.

"On the dot," I added, handing her an apple. She sniffed it and turned it around, examining it. "It's Golden Delicious," I told her. "From New Zealand, I think, or maybe France."

Agatha arched her eyebrows and sucked in her cheeks. Probably she'd never heard of New Zealand, or France. She took ages biting into it. "I have to be home at three," I warned her as she chewed, knowing how she liked to have a handle on time. I watched her polish off the whole apple, even the core. She still looked hungry, so I fished out the marshmallows. "Confectionary," I announced, feeling really pleased with myself. Then I stuck a pink one onto the end of a twig. "Ever seen this, Agatha?" Grinning, I thrust the marshmallow into the flames. Right away it blackened and drooped. "Here." I offered her the burnt goo. As she licked it I watched her face contort with the sweetness.

"It is an unexpected pleasure," she said, her little mouth puckered.

"'Yummy!' is what we say," I told her, getting the next one ready. "Or scrummy."

"Yummy, scrummy," she repeated, and laughed again.

Then me and Agatha had a bit of a picnic. She was, in her weird 1812 way, ok for an old-fashioned girl. She wouldn't drink Irn-Bru though. The very smell, she said, was ungodly! Instead she cupped up fresh snow with her hands and sucked it. It was peaceful there in the rambling old garden by the fire.

"It is wondrous." She brushed pork pie crumbs from her coat. "This could as well be 1812." She swept her arms to the sides and gazed at the garden. "Forbye Grandfather's lovely house is no more, little else here is altered."

I stared into the flames and nodded, glad Agatha couldn't see the rubbish buried under the snow. I was glad the noise of distant traffic was quieter than usual and glad there was no car alarm going off anywhere or siren screaming. "Timeless," I said, dreamily, "that's what Dad says when we go up into the hills. He says it's timeless."

6

For a while the two of us said nothing. Then Agatha placed another log on the fire, shook out her long red hair and said, "My father, Mister Albert Black, comes from a distinguished family. He has six brothers."

This seemed to be the beginning of something, and I leant back on the pillow. The clock in town struck half past two. I had a bit of listening time, if Agatha was going to tell me about 1812. "Six?" I exclaimed. "Really? Wow! That's a lot. I've not got any."

"Me neither. But Father has six. All of them successful gallant gentlemen. Some do wear monstrous large wigs. Oh, they have honours for leading men in battles in the French wars, for sailing fine merchant ships, for building spinning mills, for conducting orchestras, for keeping law and order with the militia. And every brother, you know, rides a fine thoroughbred horse. Alas poor Father, the black sheep – their success simply makes plain his failure. He tries so hard to gain their approval, but every scheme he turns his hand to ends in trouble and disappointment. He tried to become a physician but fainted at the sight of blood. He tried to make the pianoforte trill, but the gentlewomen rushed from the parlour howling like dogs. And dear Father has no horse. He has never had great luck, but now, since dear Mother died, it seems he is all at sea and canna do anything right. 'Tis dreary indeed."

I never know what to say to people if their Granddad dies. It's even worse if it's their mum. "What a shame," I muttered.

"Aye, a terrible shame indeed," she said and fell silent. For a while the two of us just stared into the flames. I thought about my mum. If she died, who would look after the twins? Dad would never manage on his own. I would have to help him. I batted the thought away and poked at the fire with a twig. "Twas three years ago she departed," Agatha continued, "and now she is with the blessed angels in heaven."

I nodded, but wasn't really sure about heaven and angels.

"Aye," Agatha went on with a sad kind of laugh, "and doubtless she is gazing down upon Mister Albert Black and shaking her pretty head. He was ever thus: a failure!"

It seemed a bit harsh to be calling your own dad a failure. "But he's probably good at some things," I protested, weakly.

Agatha nudged me in the ribs. "Ach Saul, he is a dear man and a good man, but luckless. Were it not for his wealthy brothers, especially Uncle Duncan, we'd be hiring ourselves out as servants. Twas Duncan's cutting remarks that made poor Father determined to succeed with his time travel ambitions."

"Tell me about Duncan." I was keeping her talking.

"For starters, he has the finest horse with the finest

saddle." Then Agatha grinned mischieviously, jumped to her feet, puckered her lips and threw back her head. All her sadness about her mum vanished. She winked at me, saying, "This is Duncan, Father's eldest brother." Then she patted her hand against her chest, sighed wearily and in a deep man-voice, said, "Can you triumph at nothing, brother Albert?"

"Poor Albert," I said, impressed with Agatha's acting skills. "What did he say to that?"

Agatha immediately switched characters. She thrust her hands together in a pleading style, got down on one knee and in a slower voice spoke to the imaginary brother, "Certainly Duncan. I simply havna found the particular sphere to triumph in. Have patience brother, patience. Come the day, I assure yea, the name o' Albert Black will ring out doon the lang corridors o' history. Everyone will ken me. 'Albert Black!', they will all cry and toss their bonnets high. 'Hurrah for Albert Black!' Have faith, Brother, I beseech yea!"

I cheered Agatha's performance, grinning at her, but quickly stopped when I saw her frown. "Poor Albert," I said again.

"Aye, poor indeed," Agatha plonked herself back down on the log. "For it is Uncle Duncan, you see, who gives us money. He is the richest of the family. Och, 'tis little enough, and were it not for what I can do in the kitchen and the parlour, and the little extra I bring in with my performing monkey, Father and I would be poor as vagrants. But Duncan makes much of the little he gives us."

Performing monkey? Was she having me on? Maybe

she's just a liar, that's what I thought then. I wanted to believe in her. I wanted it to be true. I wanted to believe she really did come from 1812, but part of me just couldn't. Agatha didn't notice the way I squirmed in my seat and bit my nail. She didn't notice the way I narrowed my eyes and glanced sideways at her. She just sighed and carried on.

"Alas, yea arna familiar with the name of Albert Black. So yea see, Saul. Father has failed in this too. I was to be gone but for a moment, then fly back directly with news. He so hoped time travel would give him fame. No doubt at this very moment he is on bended knee at home trying to explain to Uncle Duncan what has befallen his only child. It will be the end. Duncan already despairs of him. All the brothers do. Father has indeed fallen from grace. Now that he has lost me to the future, Duncan will have him hanged."

Agatha stared glumly into the fire. Both of us imagined the horror of Mister Albert Black swinging from a rope in the town centre. I know it sounds a bit heartless, but I was also imagining the next sentence of my essay.

Punishment was tough in the past, like you could actually get hanged for doing bad things. You would get a rope around your neck and it would kill you.

Agatha sniffed back a sob. Maybe she really was telling the truth? A tear rolled down her cheek. "Hey, Agatha," I said gently, "there's loads of famous folks I've never even heard of. I'm not that clever. To be honest, I don't know anything about history. For all I know your dad might be really well known." She flashed me a wide-eyed, hopeful look. "Don't worry, Agatha," I continued, sounding upbeat. "I'll get you back." But the next thought that flashed through my mind (though right away I felt guilty for it) was: But not yet. Hang around long enough for me to learn a few things about 1812 and win the essay! Long enough for me to win £200 and buy a bike.

Agatha seemed to cheer up. "Thanking yea, Saul," she said, smiling. "I trust yea."

"Good," I muttered, feeling bad. Of course, I wanted to help her. I wanted her dad not to get hanged. But even supposing her weird story was true, *how* was I ever going to get her back? I bit my lip, hard.

For a moment she studied a robin that was busy pecking at the pork pie crumbs. Then she went back to telling her story again. "But as yea can imagine, Saul, Father had asked for patience too many times. Duncan was losing faith in him and his hocus-pocus schemes. When last my uncle came by, their talk got quite heated and Duncan flew off the handle. They sent me to my chamber to practice my handwriting. But I heard Father when he was left, howling in sorrow."

"Poor Albert," I said for the umpteenth time. I couldn't think what else to say, but saw the next sentence of my essay in my head.

Handwriting was a great skill. Not like now when we use computers.

"Aye. Hapless indeed," she went on. "I wrote in my chamber of how sorry I felt for him, then went down to him in the parlour later. He was smoking his pipe and gazing forlornly into the flames of the fire. I said,

'Dinna fret, Father. I believe in yea,' and he took me by the hand and peered intently into my eyes. 'Child, is it true yea believe in me?' I nodded, because you see he is my father. A child must honour their parents. Father seemed on the verge of tears. He tightened the grip on my hand and said, 'Agatha, my bonny, precious lass, I wish for yea to help me.' I nodded my head, agreeing without knowing what I was agreeing to. He lowered his voice. 'I am no' like the others,' he whispered. 'My particular course to greatness doesna lie in following the customary path.' I nodded again, to encourage him. Dear Father looked so sad, so beaten. Duncan truly can belittle a person. In that moment I fervently wished for my father to succeed in something. 'It is like this, lass,' he said, dropping his voice still quieter. 'My true interests lie in things of a more metaphysical and mysterious nature.'"

Agatha paused. She could see I was confused. "He meant, Saul, that his work was no ordinary, everyday pastime. His talent lay in matters of the unseen spirit. The occult. Do yea follow?"

I nodded, not wanting to look like an idiot. "Go on!" It was quarter to three. I would have to leave soon.

"'Time,' Father explained to me, 'is the true mystery of existence. Not medicine, not music, but time.' By now, Saul, I was caught up in father's enthusiasm. Gone was the defeated look in his dark eyes. I watched in amazement. He appeared no longer the failed man but the glorious hero, famed throughout history. 'I am studying the mysterious nature of time travel,' he confided to me in a hushed voice. Lo! I knew not what to reply. I no longer understood him. But he carried on regardless. 'Aye, dear child – I wish to break doon the doors of time. I have already successfully conducted out-of-body travel, but...' At this he studied his stomach, which is quite large and round. He patted his waistcoat. 'I am too portly,' he said."

I laughed, thinking of the pillow up my hoodie. I really had to go. I loved Agatha's story and I loved the way she told it, true or not, but I was on A Mission of Trust. "Hold it there, Agatha," I said, jumping to my feet, "I really want to hear more, but I have to go. I'm in big trouble if I'm late. Here's my sleeping bag – it's a proper down one so it'll keep you really warm. Here's a pillow. And there's more food in the bag. You can stay in my den and if anybody comes snooping around just make out like you're a ghost."

"Perhaps I am," Agatha said, hanging her head, "perhaps indeed I am a lost ghost."

She was freaking me out again. I took a step back. "Agatha. Should I go and get a grown up? Should I get the police, see if they can help you? Or the social workers?"

Agatha shook her head so her ringlets swung. "No, Saul," she said. "Yea were the first person I saw, the first person I touched in this time. I lost the thread to 1812 and fastened to yea. That means we are bound together. I think it is only yea who can help me return."

"Ok..." I felt scared at all this responsibility she was piling onto me. "What about your dad? He got you lost, didn't he? He's the great time traveller."

Agatha shook her head in dismay. "No Saul. I telt yea. Father isna great. Nor is he a time traveller. Father is an apprentice, and one, I fear, who has much to learn."

"Well, it's not right. He shouldn't practise like that on his child. And he shouldn't send you off somewhere if he doesn't know how to get you back."

"Och Saul, mercy! Your mother sent yea for a message, did she not? She couldna be utterly assured of your safe return, could she? We never know what might befall us." Agatha's eyes flashed like they were on fire. There was something in her look that told me she was speaking from the heart.

"But, it's not… the same," I stammered. That tingling feeling had come back, shooting up and down my spine. A woozy feeling fuzzed my head. This girl in my den really did come from the past. I backed away. More lines from the essay spun out onto an imagined sheet of white paper.

People spoke funny two hundred years back. They ate pigeons. Men fought in the French wars.

"I have to go. And I'm sorry about leaving you on your own. But I don't know what else to do."

"I am quite happy here," Agatha said, stroking the material on my sleeping bag. "You will help me, and I am a brave lass."

"Great. And this is a good den. You'll be fine, and I'll come and get you first thing tomorrow… and…"

"And?" She gazed up at me with her pale blue eyes, twisting a coil of long hair absent-mindedly around her finger. "Then what?"

7

Yes, then what? I took a deep breath and tried to think of something. It worked. A plan flashed into my mind. If Agatha was a boy, things would be much easier. She could be one of my pals and could join the gang. She could even come to my house. Not that girls were bad, but I had never brought a girl home before and girls were not allowed to join the gang. It would look seriously weird if I suddenly brought a girl home, especially somebody who dressed like she did. I smiled at her.

"Hey, Agatha, I've got an idea. I'll bring you some proper clothes. You'll have to get rid of all that hair. I'll say you're a new boy at school. You're a good actor. You could pull it off. Then you can come to my house. You could even come to school. And you can join our gang." I nodded, all excited now. It seemed like a great plan. "You have to be a boy cause no girls are allowed in the gang. If you're going to hang around in the twenty-first century for a wee while it will make life easier. I mean, till we figure out how to get you back. At nights you can sleep here. We'll make it nice and comfy."

She gazed around, not appearing at all freaked out like I would be if it was me going to sleep in the den on my own. "It is a right bonny place," she said, then winked at me. "I am but a girl, it's true, but one used to taking care of herself. I will be grand."

"I'll bring you food," I said hurriedly. "And me and Will and Robbie will look after you, and you can tell us the next bit of the story."

She bent her head to the side and gazed up at me. "And yea will help find a way of returning me to 1812?" She spoke so quietly I could hardly hear her.

"Sure." I nodded vigorously but the truth was I had no idea where to start even thinking about that. Did she think I had special powers? Did she imagine by the twenty-first century humans had pretty much sussed everything out? Was I expected to turn into Doctor Who and build a time machine?

"Very well," said Agatha, smiling and looking a whole lot happier, "I will pretend to be a boy of the future, and yea will assist me in my return home." She lifted her hand up for me to shake it. I did, then turned, ran up the garden and dashed through the hole in the hedge. I hurried over the wasteland, then sprinted, slithered and slid all the way home.

I burst through the front door just as the church bells clanged three o'clock. I had made it!

Later, in my room, when I lay on my beanbag worrying just how I was supposed to get a girl back to history, I wondered if bells could be part of my time machine? I still had that 1p left of Milky Way change. I went to the window, opened it and leant out. I knew our tiny back garden wasn't the river Tweed, but figured wishes are wishes. I tossed the coin into the snow.

"I wish that I can help get Agatha Black home. And I wish that I win the history prize so I can get a bike."

And while I was at it, and because three seemed like a wishing kind of number, I whispered into the night, "And I wish Crow would back off and stop threatening me, so I don't have to be scared anymore."

That evening, still Saturday, 15th December, while Mum was putting the twins to bed and Dad was out working (because Saturday nights before Christmas are his absolutely busiest time), I got busy finding disguise clothes for Agatha.

As per usual, I had no credit on my phone, but I was allowed ten free texts at weekends so I sent Will and Robbie a message.

SOS. Gang meeting 2moro 2pm in den.
TOP SECRET.

Then I found a thick red hoodie, a pair of blue trousers and a black t-shirt. I laid them out ready, next to the scissors. I could hear mum making herself a cup of tea in the kitchen. I nipped through to tell her I was going to stay in my room and read my history book because I was going to have a go at the history competition.

"Is this my son we're talking about?" she said, cheekily. "Can this possibly be Saul Martin, who avoids homework more determinedly than any child I know?"

"Aw, Mum, give me a break. I've always been kinda interested in history."

"Really?" She raised her eyebrows to the ceiling. Then she smiled and gave me a hug, turning all soft and mumsy. "Sorry, sausage. That's terrific you like history. I didn't know. But hey, if I can help with your essay, just ask."

"Thanks Mum," I said, and I made a funny face at the twins before dashing back to my room. So far, so good.

My phone was beeping.

> **Can't, got to visit Grandad.**

That was from Will.

> **Can't. Going to winter wonderland. Yo!**

That was from Robbie.

I felt miffed. If Will was any kind of proper gang member he'd wriggle out of visiting his grandad. What a wimp! And if Robbie was any kind of friend, like he always said he was, he'd invite me to Winter Wonderland too! I would love to go to Winter Wonderland. Every year I wanted to go to Winter Wonderland, and every year Mum said she'd think about it, but did we ever go? No. And now the twins had arrived, we never would. I picked up a ragged old teddy and threw it across the room, remembering how, every year, Robbie told me how fab it was and how he skated like a pro and went on the big wheel and ate candy floss and hotdogs and loads of sweets. This year was going to be the same.

45

I started to feel sorry for myself, until I remembered Agatha. Compared with her I was fine. I gazed out the window. The moon and stars were out. I felt pretty guilty leaving her in the den, but what else could I have done? I wouldn't sleep there on my own for a thousand pounds. 1812 children were pretty brave. That could go in the essay.

Children back two hundred years ago were braver than children of today's modern world. They didn't have lights so they got used to the dark.

Sure, I was angry with them, but I knew there was no way Robbie was going to give up his trip to Winter Wonderland. So I texted back.

How about 10 am?

They both texted back

Will try

What a gang! Here was me, the leader, ready to let them in on the biggest secret of the century, of two or three centuries actually, and they say, wimpishly: will try!

Me and Dad usually do our thing on Sunday mornings (unless he has to take somebody to the airport). While Mum fusses over the twins, Dad makes a fry-up, then after breakfast me and Dad usually have a kick about. I wondered how Agatha would be in goals? My plan was to get up early the next day, rush over to the den, turn Agatha into a boy then bring her (him) back for breakfast.

I fell asleep as soon as my head hit the pillow then didn't wake up till half past seven. It was still dark outside. Lying there all groggy with sleep, I couldn't quite believe in the time-traveller's daughter. But then I saw the blue jeans, red hoodie and scissors laid out on the floor.

I got up and pulled my clothes on. I glanced out to the street. Dad's taxi stood in an orange pool of light. The snow hadn't melted during the night and across the road in Sam's garden I could see the eerie silhouette of a snowman. I didn't like thinking too much about Sam. He was ok, but Crow was his cousin. Crow stole kids' pocket money. He dropped litter and didn't care if anyone saw him. He'd been banned from every shop in Peebles. Once he let down the tyres of Dad's taxi, and if he spied me he made his eyes like evil slits and ran his finger across his throat. He was seriously bad news. And what had I ever done to him? Nothing! Robbie said he picked on boys who didn't have big brothers. Robbie said Crow didn't need reasons. Some folk just annoyed him! I wasn't exactly thrilled, thinking about going up to high school. If Crow found out about the den, he would trash it, for sure.

Dad said for me to ignore him. Trying hard not to think about him, I stuffed Agatha's clothes into a rucksack. I slipped the scissors down the side pocket then scribbled a note in the kitchen for Dad.

Hi dad, gone sledging. Snow might melt soon. Don't want to miss it. I'll be back for breakfast. Maybe bring a mate if that's ok? Saul.

Then I went out. When I reached the laundrette I hovered for a while, checking the coast was clear. Once I was sure no one was lurking in any doorways, I made a mad dash up the lane and over the wasteland. I was excited. This was the biggest adventure of my life so far. It felt great to be out as the sun was coming up. The sky was pink and the black branches of the trees were like long witchy fingers. My footsteps crunched down in the snow. Forget Robbie's expensive Winter Wonderland. I was in the real thing, and it was magical.

8

As I got closer to the hedge I kept an eye out for signs of a fire, but there was no curl of smoke. I was halfway through the hedge when I heard the sound of Agatha singing. I stopped and listened.

"*In dulce jubilo*, sing with hearts aglow…" She had a beautiful clear voice.

Without rustling the holly, I stepped out into the garden. The singing was coming from inside the den. I took a few steps over the snow, waited till there was a pause in her song, then knocked on the door of Pisa. The singing stopped. "It's me," I called in a loud whisper, "Saul."

"Good morning, Saul," she called from inside the den. "Please enter."

I did, and what a surprise. She'd made the wee place like a real home. Somehow she'd managed to gather up the embers from her fire and now they glowed in a little tin plate in the middle of the floor. It was so warm in there. She'd even brought in some branches from the evergreen tree and put them about the den for decorations. It felt really Christmassy. She was sitting up in my sleeping bag with just her head popping out. She had taken off her flouncy hat and her long curly hair spilled down almost to the ground. I swallowed hard, thinking how I planned to cut it all off.

"Did you sleep ok, Agatha?" I plonked down on one of the stone seats.

"What is ok?"

"It means alright. Fine. Cool." I racked my brains to think of what the O and K actually stood for.

"Majestically well," she said, "and I wasna alone."

"What?"

She saw my startled expression and laughed. "Three wee broon shrews snuggled up with me," she explained, "and then, the most stupendous visitor – a young roe deer rubbed its head against the door in the middle of the night. I admitted him and in he trotted. The poor creature was that frozen. He curled down at my feet and slept there till the dawn. So I was warm as toast, in right pleasant company, and not a whit afeart."

"Oh! Right. Great! It's just, I was kind of worried about you." I felt more than a bit miffed that all the time me, Robbie and Will had been in the den we'd never seen a deer. "I thought you might have been really scared."

"Och no, Saul. Dinna fret on account of me." She reached over and patted me on the hand. "If I needs must remain in the future for a few days, while we are planning my return, then at least I have this fine wee house. And remember – this is my grandfather's garden. Nothing terrible can befall me in Grandfather's garden. His spirit will watch over me."

"Great. Anyway, Agatha," I said, thinking how we better crack on with business, "I bought you some clothes." I rummaged in the bag and pulled them out. "This way you'll look normal and folk won't get suspicious." I handed them to her. "So I'll just go outside and you can put them on."

Agatha stared at the jeans like they might bite her. At the risk of sounding obvious I said, "You put your legs in there, and zip up."

"Zip up?"

I mimed pulling a zip, with a zzzzzzip noise for effect. "Then," I went on, "you put the t-shirt on and the hoodie. It's pretty straightforward." I stepped out into the garden, leaving her to get on with it. It was light now and the low sun slanted onto the snow, making it peachy coloured.

"Yea may enter," Agatha called after a few minutes. I did and what a change! She'd put the hoodie on the wrong way, with the hood like a bib under her chin. The trousers seemed a bit big, but apart from that she was beginning to look normal. I picked up the scissors and snapped them shut in the air. Agatha winced.

"We should get this bit over and done with quick." I took a step towards her. She screamed and ducked. "Chill," I said, "I'm not going to stab you. I'm only going to cut your hair."

She clutched at her hair. It was longer than any hair I'd ever seen. It must have taken years to grow. "Hey, relax, it'll be fine, and it means we don't need to hide you away." I gabbled on, trying to make this sound like a great idea. "You can come to my house for breakfast. Cause, the thing is, I don't exactly have friends who are girls, but I've got loads of friends who are boys.

You'll just be one of them. That way, nobody will think anything of it." I took another small step towards her. "It's not that there's anything wrong with girls. It's just, we don't have any in the gang." I lifted the scissors into the air, and smiled.

"So," she said, staring wide-eyed at my sharp weapon, "well-made bucks in your time dinna have tresses?"

"Well-made what?"

"Bucks. Boys. Oh help!" She sunk her head into the hood and her muffled cries of "No, Saul, I beg yea," really got to me. I didn't know what to do. I didn't want to be cruel. She'd asked me to help. So here I was, trying to help and it was freaking her out. I sighed loudly and flopped down onto the floor, waiting for her to drop the hood.

She whimpered. "When I take Pug onto the market square for him to do his tricks I also make as if I am a boy. I twist my hair up into a tweed cap. I smudge my face with dirt." She lowered the hood and peeked out. "Have yea no tweed cap?"

"That won't work, Agatha. Anybody could pull the cap off. And anyway, I don't have one."

I heard her take a deep shuddering breath. "In that case, I agree. Forgive me for being in a frightful temper." Slowly she shook out her hair. "Yea are in the right. I am in a fearful predicament that requires desperate measures. Caring for my tresses is but idle vanity, and vanity is a great folly." She gathered her hair and swept it back, thrusting out her jaw with determination. "Cut it off," she ordered, then shut her eyes tight.

I hadn't thought about a style. I took a long curl. It felt silky between my fingers. I took a deep breath and chopped it off level with her ear. The scissors weren't very sharp but I kept going, hacking and snipping. Bit by bit the long red hair floated down and all the time Agatha sobbed quietly. She kept her eyes closed. Eventually all the long hair was gone and she now had a fairly messy cropped hairstyle. I took a step back and examined her, like I'd seen real hairdressers do. Yep, she was beginning to look normal.

"Finished," I announced, trying to sound chirpy. Agatha wiped her tears and opened her eyes. "It's pretty smart," I said. "In a messy kind of way." I wasn't joking, it really was, but Agatha didn't seem convinced. I smiled at her. "It's… er… short," I said, lamely. "And… nice, and…"

She stared at the red hair on the dirt floor while I ran out of things to say. Slowly she brought her hands to her head and patted her short hair. "It is done," she said, "and now I will need a boy's name."

"Yeah. I'd been thinking about that. How about Gareth?" I suggested, pushing the cut hair away with my foot.

Agatha shook her head. "Randolph," she declared. "It is my absolutely favourite name. I have always dreamt of being Randolph."

Randolph sounded as old fashioned as Agatha. "What do they call you when you take your performing monkey out?" I asked her.

"Monkey boy." She frowned. "And that is no proper name for anyone. No, if I am to be a boy, I will be

Randolph!" She looked so eager. Personally I didn't like the name one bit, but it was obvious she adored it. "Ok," I agreed, putting the scissors back into the rucksack. "And another thing, Randolph, if I'm going to show you to the world, you're going to have to speak like me. Or folks are going to guess you're from the past."

Agatha shook her head and rolled up the sleeping bag. "No Saul. People might imagine I hail from a strange place, or have curious manners – but they willna guess I come from history." She grinned at me, and with all that long curly hair gone she did look boyish. "But dinna fret. I will make every effort to appear normal. I will model myself on yea."

"Well, for a start, it's *you*, Agatha, not *yea*." Then I laughed, not sure that modelling herself on me was the best idea, but kind of liking it at the same time. I made myself comfy by the little fire. We still had an hour before Will and Robbie turned up. And two hours before I was expected back for food. Dad would just be getting up now. He'd see the note. And he'd set an extra place. Everything was going to plan. And now that the hairdressing thing was over, we could chat. I'd been wanting to hear more of her time travel story. "So, Randolph," I said, "tell me more, like yesterday. Your father told you time travel was his path to greatness. And you said you'd help him, right?"

"Yes, poor Father," she said, "He needed help from someone. My first time-travel experiment took place when I was eleven years old." She sighed and her whole body shuddered. I felt more than a bit spooked.

9

Agatha sat on the pillow and gazed into the orange embers. She was, I noticed, still wearing her 1812 black lace-up boots but, considering they were 200 years old, they were quite like boots you'd find in shops today. She looked pretty cool, except that she still had the hoodie on the wrong way.

She turned to me and sighed again. "Yes, Saul," she said, "the first experiment was last summer, six months ago."

"You mean two hundred years and six months ago?"

Agatha frowned. "I suppose so. Well, in any case, in our house, Father has a study. I have a fondness for the place. It is full of clocks and contraptions for measuring time. He also has vials for water. Father allows me to wander into his study, even when he isna there. He knows I adore playing with the water."

I felt a pang of pity for her. The essay kicked off in my head.

Children two hundred years ago didn't have anything like as many toys as us. They played with water.

Agatha wrinkled her nose and laughed, again spookily reading my thoughts. "You see little joy in water? Ach, Saul, it is wondrous great. Especially the water lovingly collected from the river Tweed and now kept in Father's study. I see many grand images on its surface."

She's mad. That's what shot through my mind. She's off her head.

Agatha went on, growing excited. "Aye, water is a happy pastime. Even better is playing with my monkey, or teaching him new tricks." Agatha paused and smiled fondly into the distance. "Dearest Pug. I miss him so."

"Right. Um, Agatha, I was going to ask you about that. Are you serious? You've actually got a pet monkey?"

"Indeed I have. Pug can be a rogue at times. Ach, he will be searching high and low for me now. On busy market days, Pug and his antics bring in a good shilling or even two. Oh Saul, yea should see his tricks. He can smoke a pipe!"

"Really?"

"Aye, a clay pipe. He puffs away, quite the thing. The folks love it. They throw farthings and I scoop them up and gather them in my pocket."

I laughed, trying to imagine what they'd say about a smoking pet in our health and wellbeing lessons at school. "Well, it must be pretty amazing to have a monkey," I said. "You're lucky. I don't even have a guinea pig. We had a goldfish once, but it died."

Agatha looked as if she might burst into tears. I don't know if she was sad at my dead goldfish, or if she was missing her monkey. "Anyway," I hurried on, "you didn't do the time travel experiment on Pug."

"Heavens no!" Agatha frowned. "On no account is my monkey allowed in Father's study. Yea see, there are many candles burning in there. Father is afeart Pug could start a fire."

"Seriously?"

"Hand on my heart, Saul. It is true."

The stupid giggles had taken hold of me, though a burning house and burning monkey weren't exactly a laughing matter. Agatha, who thankfully seemed to have a sense of humour, laughed too. "Then where would I be, Saul?" she said, her face all flushed with mirth. "If the house were to burn down together with all Father's contraptions, I would surely never return!"

"You could hang out here, I suppose?"

But Agatha shook her head. "No Saul. I must return. I have my life to live. I will tell yea what I understand of time travel. If yea are to help return me to 1812, yea will need to learn something of this abnormal art. Yea will become the apprentice!"

"You, Agatha. I told you. It's *you*, not *yea*."

Agatha knitted her brows then smiled. "Beg your pardon: you," she said. "*You* heed well. Father calls upon the elements. There are seven of them. And they must all be in harmony. So in the study Father collects earth and water, air and fire. And I – the experiment – must be surrounded by these elements."

This was getting interesting and scientific. She went on, growing excited. "You see, Saul, the air element must be turned to vapour. Father has been experimenting with different kinds of vapours."

I frowned. "Steam," she explained, "and Father can colour the vapours blue and red."

"How?" I asked.

"He suspends a glass globe by the one small window in the study. It catches the sunlight. The colour glances off the glass and colours the vapours. Then there is the element of gold. This, alas, is costly and father scrimps on this. But, so he tells me, the vibration of gold will protect me as I travel through time." Agatha laughed sadly and shook her head. "The fleck he gave me was that small I couldna even feel it."

I could see tears well up in Agatha's blue eyes. She rubbed them with the back of her hand, took another deep breath then carried on. "As I understand it, all these elements – earth, vapours, water, fire and gold – are set in motion by the sixth element. This, Saul, is an antique song. The song causes a shudder in the air."

I raised an eyebrow. "Shudder?"

"A crack in the atmosphere. Through which I slip, alas." She buried her face in her hands.

"It's ok, Agatha," I said chirpily. "I'll help. But you said there were seven elements. What's the seventh?"

"Yew. The yew tree." Agatha gazed at me to make sure I understood. I nodded, impatiently. Sure, I knew about yew trees. You got them in graveyards and they looked witchy. "I press my feet upon wood hewn from the ancient yew," she went on. "I gaze at the almanac on the study wall. On this first occasion, it said July 18, 1812. Throughout the ritual, Father chanted his ancient tune. Then, well, the only way I can faithfully describe the next part is to say it was like someone in the far distance calling my name. I found myself rushing down a long black tunnel towards them. Then suddenly the voice stopped."

Annoyingly Agatha stopped too and stared into the glowing embers. "Don't stop there!" I said, practically biting her head off, "Tell me what happened next!"

"To be frank, not a great deal. I blinked several times, to rid myself of the buzzing in my head – like a bee it was. Coming to, I found myself in the same place and Father was still there, though the contraptions were not. His beard was bushier. His waistcoat, I noted, had two buttons missing. I felt bewildered. I saw the almanac on the wall behind him. It was turned to July 18, 1813. The room was the same, and yet not the same. I had faded in 1812 and in the twinkling of an eye had reappeared one year into the future. Then instantly I felt my head spin.

"The song called me back again. I felt a great rushing force pull me down that black tunnel. And once more I was in what Father calls 'current time'. He was punching the air for joy. The buttons were back on his waistcoat. The almanac said July 18, 1812. Sun streamed through the window.

"'Success!' shouted Father, beaming from ear to ear, as if he had a feather in his cap. 'Aye, dear child. What you behold before yea is nothing less than majestic success!'

"I wandered upstairs to my chamber, though I felt somewhat shaken up. Through the morning, I could hear Father shouting, 'Yes! Yes! I have broken down the doors of time! YES! I am famous at last! I am…'"

"But Agatha," I interrupted, "if he managed to get you back then, why didn't he get you back this time?"

Agatha wrung her hands and chewed her lip.

"Vaulting ambition," she murmured. And before I could ask what that meant she went on. "It is like a swelling of the head. From that day forth, Father grew blind with ambition. He thought he could achieve anything he set his mind to. And though time travel frightened me, it also fascinated me. And yea know, I so wanted Father to be skilled at something. He had succeeded in transporting me a year hence. I believed in him. But after that successful experiment he was not content with small time transportations. Ach no. 'One year is small fry, Agatha,' he said, puffing out his chest. So he locked himself in his study, intent on frying the biggest fish. Strange noises and smells came from that place. Sometimes, while I was busy in the kitchen, scrubbing potatoes or cleaning the floor, Father would hasten to me and say, 'I am close, Agatha. So close to the biggest time-shifting experiment the world has ever known. It succeeded before. It will succeed again. But this time, child – if yea agree to help me in my work – yea will travel far into the future. Ach, the sights yea will see. The changes yea will behold. No more scrubbing tatties. Yea'll be a great explorer. Say yea agree, Agatha!'"

"And?" I was perched on the edge of my stone seat. Of course, I knew the answer.

"Certainly I was much agitated. I would have been content being a normal child, playing with my pet monkey, saying my prayers, sewing, dancing, reading, but..."

"But what?"

"But, life was often dreary. I wasna a normal child. I was forced to beg for farthings with Pug on the street.

And, as Father said, his experiment in time travel succeeded before, so I trusted it would again." Then Agatha grinned widely. "And in addition, I am a girl who dearly loves adventures. So I agreed and we shook hands on it. 'Tis all true," Agatha said, "each and every word."

"Sure," I replied. She believed it, that was for sure, but I wasn't discounting the possibility that she was bonkers. I didn't know what was true and what was false. "Sure," I said again, not sure of anything.

10

Snow began to fall outside. Me and Agatha sat opposite each other, gazing into the glowing embers. I was drawn into another world by Agatha's story telling. Plus I had loads more for my essay. My head was full of history.

In 1812, girls learnt about sewing and dancing and if you were rich you had a horse with a saddle, and calendars were called almanacs. Also fire could be a big problem because there were lots of candles, and they probably didn't have fire engines.

"Keep going, Agatha," I said, "tell me more about helping your dad."

She gazed above my head, like she was seeing way past me, and whispered, "Blue, red and yellow steam coils about me. I stand motionless in the middle of Father's cramped, low-ceilinged study. The coloured steam swirls faster. Sweeps by my unblinking eyes. Merges with my coppery hair, turning it red then yellow then blue."

Agatha pressed her hand against her chest, then carried on. "At my feet a ring of objects enclose me. From a wooden rafter above the window a glass globe hangs down, catching the low winter sunbeams and flashing them blue, red and yellow into the room."

She looked far away. "My right hand, clenched in a fist, trembles." As she said this I saw she was acting it out. "Perspiration heats my forehead. My hair sticks to my temples. My eyes stare ahead, as though into some longed for future."

She was so intense, I was getting freaked. "Hey, Agatha?"

She shook her head and snapped out of her memories. "Ach, the truth is Saul," she stared at me through the flames, "ever since Father spoke of the far future I yearned for it. I thought about it often. I wondered if children would be the same. I questioned if the world would be greatly changed. I so longed to travel. I have only journeyed once to Edinburgh town and it was such a wondrous place... But we have no carriage. Not as much as a lame horse do we have. I would so love to behold the very grand cathedral there of Saint Giles. Ach, I have seen so little of the world."

"Maybe I could show you around. We could go places. See things."

Agatha beamed at me. "I should like that greatly. Thank you."

"But you still haven't said what Albert was doing. Was he singing or something? If I'm the apprentice now, I have to know."

Agatha's pale blue eyes widened again, the way they did when she was remembering her home. "Ah, Saul, if I was a picture of stillness, the one other person in the study, my dear father, couldna keep still. 'Yes!' he shouted, punching the air. 'The time is right, my dear Agatha.' He laughed and clapped his chubby hands together. 'I feel it in my bones!' He fixed his gaze on the hands of the clock that were creeping loudly towards ten. He fell to his knees and nudged the plate of earth closer, then swirled the water in the bowl with a poker. He pushed the yew branch closer so it pressed against my feet. 'Touch the ancient yew, my dear. Aye, that's it! That's it! Let its ageless spirit guide you.' Then he rose to his feet, wiping his brow with a large handkerchief. He whipped out his pocket watch, swaying restlessly from foot to foot."

"And what happened?"

"By this time the coloured vapours fair filled up the room. 'All is in place,' Father announced, clapping again. He placed himself outside the magic circle. 'Feel the gold. It will protect yea. Surely, it will.'

"Saul, it was then I did feel the very heart in me jolt. Yea see, I couldna actually feel the gold. The fleck I'd been given was no bigger than a flea. I did try. Oh, I tried so very hard to feel the gold. My fist shook. My palm sweated.

"'Soon you will be the best travelled young lady in the land,' Father shouted, heedless of my agitation. "Ah! What scenes you will behold. Take note. Look well around yea, then haste yea back and tell me all. Fare yea well, lassie. Fare yea well.' Father cleared his throat. The clock whirred. The coloured steam intensified. He pulled at his moustache then with a quavering voice, broke into song.

"The notes of the haunting tune swirled around me. I felt the hardness of the branch press against the toe caps of my boots. Sight and sound blurred. I was already far gone. No longer could I tell which was steam, which was song. All was a blur. The seven flickering candle flames sputtered and mingled with the rippling water. The clock struck ten. The glass globe swung or was it the earth? Small rainbows slid across the room. The room slid. But where was the gold?

"The song grew fainter. The light dimmed until I beheld only shadows. My eyelids grew heavy. My chin dropped. I grew weightless. Wind, at first a whistle, then a gale, blew through me. It moved me. It pushed me.

"Then it started to snow. The great wind ceased. Everything grew white. What peace then! I had come into a white and new world. It was marvellous. I felt filled with excitement and was ready to open my eyes when suddenly a brash noise clattered into the white peace: a thundering, roaring, screeching, terrifying noise! I grew much afeart. Then, dear good Saul, yea found me!" She dropped her head and looked into the glowing embers. "That is my tale. That is how I became transported."

Agatha fell silent as if there was nothing left to say. I opened my mouth but shut it again. I stared at her. I had never seen anyone look so lost. Her eyes filled up with tears. We both stared into the embers of the fire. I felt that shiver again. This mysterious girl sitting opposite me in the den really did come from the past. I watched as she went to wind her long hair around her finger. Except, of course, she didn't have long hair anymore. She frowned then pulled at her earlobe instead.

"Alas," she said, breaking the silence, "I found myself in a most dangerous place. Yea saw me. I was standing on the road and there burst in all of a sudden a terrific commotion so that I lost all my concentration. I lost hold of the thread that held me to 1812. I lost the gold."

"It was a car, Agatha. You almost got yourself knocked down by a car."

"Acar." She shuddered.

"No. A. Car. It was heading straight for you. You almost died." I sat up, thinking I could hear a rustle in the distance. "Hey, Randolph. My gang could show up any minute. Maybe you should turn your hoodie so this hood bit is at the back."

"There is so much to learn," she said, twisting it round. Now that she was properly dressed and her hair was short she looked like a normal boy.

"So, they'll be here soon. How are you doing, Randolph?"

"Fair to middling," she replied, sniffing away what was left of her tears. "And are yea – begging your pardon, *you* – are *you* going to tell your gang the truth about me?"

Just at that moment the five secret code knocks came rapping on the door. "Dunno," I mumbled, then shouted out, "Who goes there?"

"Gang member Robbie."

"Gang member Will."

I took a deep breath, flung back my shoulders and shouted out, "Enter!"

11

"We haven't got much time," Will and Robbie chorused as they stepped into the den. They both spotted Agatha at the same time and jostled for a better view. I sat on the stone, waiting for them to say something. Will, I noticed, looked annoyed. He had wanted his pal Lewis to join the gang but I had said three was a good number for a gang and plus there wasn't much room in the den. I guessed that was what was bothering him.

"Thought you said three..."

Robbie joined in, "...was a good number for a gang?"

Agatha had flicked up her hood so her face was half in shadow. I could see her eyes flit from Will to Robbie and back again. I stood up and took command. "Look guys, this is an emergency. This is Randolph. Randolph, that's Will. And that's Robbie." Agatha stood up and thrust her hand out to shake hands. Robbie, true to form, laughed, while Will managed to turn the handshake into a high-five.

"Well, it's not fair," whined Robbie, throwing me his best scowl.

But I didn't miss a beat. "Fair? You're off to Winter Wonderland and I'm not. That's what's not fair. And don't forget, I'm the gang leader."

Robbie made a big deal of chewing his gum. So far Agatha hadn't opened her mouth. Will made a little hrrmph noise, like he was in the huff, so I made up my mind there and then not to mention time travel. They weren't mature enough. And, the thought did rip through my mind that they were better at writing than me, and they might enter the history essay competition – and win!

"Randolph is on ze run," I hissed, in my Russian spy accent. "He needs to lie low for wee while so I tell him we good guys – we give him safe place. No problem!"

"Wow!" said Robbie.

"Wow!" echoed Will.

"Yeah, that's right," I said, "double wow. Poor Randolph's a bit shaken up. He overheard his parents say how they were going to pack him off to some boarding school, so he didn't hang around. He's really brave. Randolph slept the whole night in the den – on his own."

Robbie and Will started to look seriously impressed. Never in a billion years would they spend even half an hour in the den on their own at night. "No way?" they both said, gaping at Agatha. She nodded her head but was obviously not trusting herself to speak. Which gave me another idea.

"Randolph's lost his voice."

Agatha looked relieved. I carried on, amazed I was such an imaginative storyteller all of a sudden. "Yeah, the shock of running away, after being locked in a cupboard under the stairs, has left her, I mean *him*, speechless."

Robbie eyed me suspiciously, narrowing his eyes. "Like, how come you know all this then?"

"He wrote it all down," I blurted out, then quickly added, "and cause we got cold we burnt the paper."

"Randolph actually slept under the stairs? Wow! So, Randolph is like… Harry Potter?" Will asked.

"Yeah… something like that. And you both have to swear on the old tree that you'll keep dead quiet. Ok? It'll be like an adventure," I went on. "And it's only for a few days. Just till Randolph decides what he wants to do next. Eh, Randolph?"

Agatha's eyes widened, as if I was speaking a foreign language. I nodded my head. Thankfully she got my drift and copied me.

Will and Robbie were won round. I could tell. "Ok," said Will, "I can bring him a few sausage rolls, and sweets. And he can have my torch."

"And I've got magazines and crosswords and paper and stuff like that," Robbie said, smiling at Agatha. "It'll give you something to do, Randolph."

Agatha smiled up at them both. "I told you you'd be welcome in our gang, Randolph," I said, relieved.

Then me, Robbie and Will went down to the old tree to swear an oath of silence. We went round the back of the tree, out of sight. "This is getting pretty exciting," said Will, pressing the palm of his hand against the gnarled trunk. "So, is runaway Randolph in our gang then?"

"For a wee while," I replied, cupping my hand over Will's. Robbie pressed his hand over mine. "Eyes closed," I said and we stayed quiet like that for a few seconds. When we opened our eyes and pulled our hands away, I saw down low on the bark the worn, carved initials $A\!B$ staring out at us.

"A.B., see that? That's old. I wonder who A.B. was?" Robbie whispered.

Just then a twig snapped behind us. We all swung round and there stood Agatha Black. She smiled and I saw her gaze flick to the carved initials.

The church bells rang out for quarter to eleven. "Yo! Winter Wonderland, here I come," Robbie yelled, running off. "I'll tell you all about it guys!" And he was gone. That left Will who seemed more nervous when Robbie wasn't by his side.

"Right then," he said, "I better get going too." Agatha was still gaping at the tree. I grabbed Will by the elbow and steered him away from her.

"I forgot my hat," Will said. He pushed open the creaking old shed door. I followed him into the den and saw him bend to pick up his hat, then stare at the locks of long red hair on the ground. I'd kicked them into the corner, but I'd forgotten to hide them completely. My mind went blank. I couldn't think of one decent lie to account for the hair. But Will didn't mention it. He just picked up his hat, gave me a confused stare, then left.

"Thanks Will," I shouted after him. "Thanks for helping Randolph out. Have a good time at your grandad's."

Then he was gone. First thing I did was burn the hair, which completely stank out the den. But then I noticed Agatha's dress folded up neatly in the corner of the shed. Had Will noticed that too? Then I thought of Dad. He'd be setting a place for my new mate, and stirring the beans and buttering the toast and Mum would be feeding the twins and saying, "Where's Saul?"

I dashed outside. Agatha was still staring at the tree. She was shaking her head slowly from side to side. I jumped when she spoke – I'd got used to her having no voice. "I carved my initials here in the summer. Grandfather lent me his sharp knife. He said the tree would bear my stamp for a long, long time. Indeed, he was correct."

That confirmed it. Agatha Black was for real. She really did come from 1812. She wasn't crazy. I felt dizzy. Maybe it was me that was mad? "Hey, Randolph," I said, tugging gently at her sleeve. "It's time for some food and I'm really hungry. Let's go."

But Agatha pulled away. "This is the tree that will help transport me." She placed her hands on the gnarled old bark. "Yea could make the vapours turn bright. Yea could protect me with gold. Yea could chant the ancient song, then I can leave."

Do I look like the kind of person whose bedroom is filled with gold? I thought, but I didn't want to dishearten her. "It might take a while to get all of that together, Agatha. And meanwhile you can check out life now. I can show you around."

"Yea are kind to me, Saul," she said, smiling. "And yea are right. Yea have not learnt the art yet, and I dinna wish to be hurled back to the wrong time." She stepped back from the tree and came up to me. "Of course, I wish to learn of your time and see the world. It is only that, the bond to my home being broken, I am afeart I am lost forever. The longer I am in the future the more difficult it may be to return to the past. And there is Father to think of. And dearest Pug."

The truth was, I didn't want Agatha Black to go rushing off back to her time, even if I had known how to get her there. It wasn't just that I wanted more history for my essay. There was something about her, and this adventure. I felt more excited that I'd been for ages. "I hope your father's ok," I said.

"Yes, we must pray we can succeed and Father is not hanged. Will you pray?"

"Sure," I said. Praying was like wishing, wasn't it? It was more or less the same thing. I'd already wished. I could wish again.

Agatha looked relieved. She patted me on the shoulder. "Oh, dear Saul. I always longed for a real friend. Is it not amusing that I must travel two hundred years in order to find one?"

I didn't know what to say. I smiled at her. At the same time my stomach rumbled. "Hey, Randolph, have you ever heard of bacon and eggs?"

"As a matter of fact, Saul," she said, laughing, "I have." Then she dashed up the garden and into the den. I ran after her and stood in the doorway, watching as she bent over the fire and scooped up grey ash, scattering it over the glowing embers. "This is smooring," she explained. "It saves the warmth and makes fire safe, in case yea – I mean *you* – are interested." That done, she skipped out of the den.

I scratched my head and wondered whether Agatha, as well as being a time traveller, was also a mind reader?

She was always answering my thoughts. "Come on!" I shouted, "I'm starved," and dashed through the gap in the hedge. Agatha followed.

As we sped over the snowy field I struggled to keep up with her. She was a girl. She was skinny. And she was fast. She clambered over the wall like she was mounting a horse. Panting hard I suggested she keep her voice lost for a wee while longer, until she got used to twenty-first-century speech.

"Certainly, I will remain mute if that makes everything smoother," she said, running up the lane, not out of breath at all.

As I ran, puffing and panting, I wrote the next few essay sentences in my head.

Scottish children two hundred years ago were fast runners. They had no cars of course so they used their legs a lot. And they said words like dreary and afeart and well-made buck, which means a fit guy, and some of them even had monkeys as pets. And they didn't travel much. The girls I mean, not the monkeys. Again this was because of cars.

I was going to win. I was sure of it. I could practically feel the £200 in my hands. We reached my street. I hurried towards the house with Randolph at my side. At the garden gate I could smell crispy bacon waiting for me. I glanced at Agatha and saw her little nose twitch. But then her face clouded and she reached out and took my hand. "Do yea not hate as I do how the swine squeal so when we are obliged to kill them?"

Squealing swine? I pushed opened the gate. "Yeah, sure," I quipped, panting. "We've got a whole pigsty round the back. And a monkey in the house swinging from the light bulbs."

Her eyes lit up. "How delightful," she trilled. "I miss my pet monkey so much. But yea have one too! Yea didna say."

"Only joking, Randolph. You only get monkeys in the zoo nowadays." Her face fell. She really did miss her pipe-smoking Pug. "Right, Randolph," I said, my hand on the door handle and my heart skipping a beat, "here goes, and remember, leave all the talking to me."

12

I pushed the front door open, muttered, "Hey-ho, here-we-go," and stepped onto the Welcome Home mat. Agatha was kicking her boots against the front step to shake the snow free. "I'm back," I shouted, pulling her in. Agatha, her eyes wide as saucers, gazed around the hallway. She reached out to touch the photograph on the wall of five-year-old me, first day in my school uniform. Then she jumped in fright at a large plastic rose in a glass vase. She shuddered at the whiteness of the light bulb above her head. "Agatha," I hissed, "don't look so surprised at everything, ok?"

Agatha bit her lip and nodded, her blue eyes like a rabbits in headlights. "Ok," she whispered back.

"Right. Just do what I do." I nudged the kitchen door open with my elbow, a big smile ready and heart beating fast. Mum was sitting at the table with a crying Esme in one arm and Ellie in the other. She was about to say something, when I leapt in with my next storytelling performance.

"Hi, Mum. Sorry I'm late. You'll so never guess what happened. I was sledging on Randolph's – oh, by the way, this is Randolph, and I was on his sledge.

We veered off course and crashed bang into a thorny hedge. Well, the good news is we're ok, but we lost the sledge. Anyway I invited Randolph back for breakfast. You're always saying how you like to see who I'm hanging out with. And poor Randolph – his parents are away at some convention today. They *trust* him." I flashed her a look. "And he's kind of just hanging about, so I brought him home. Oh, and he just got his tonsils out, so he can't speak."

Through all this super-fast speech, Mum was examining Agatha, Dad was dishing out breakfast and Agatha was gaping at the twins who had stopped crying and were gazing straight at her.

"Great to meet you, Randolph," Dad said, slopping beans onto a plate. "A friend of Saul's is always welcome. I hope you like beans?"

I made a tiny nod of my head. Agatha did the same. "Good lad," Dad said. "Now why don't you come and sit down."

"Convention?" Mum was staring at Randolph. "What kind of convention?"

I didn't miss a beat. "Model trains," I said and smiled at Agatha who promptly smiled back.

"Takes all sorts," I heard Mum mutter under her breath. She spooned up mashed banana then stared at Agatha's clothes. "Those look familiar," she said.

"Me and Randolph like the same style." I hastily patted the seat next to me. Agatha took the hint and sat down. As she did, Ellie let out a whopper of a scream and that, I can tell you, was music to my ears. It distracted Mum and gave Agatha a chance to relax.

I made a big deal of picking up my cutlery, hoping she would copy me and not start tearing the food with her hands.

But I didn't need to worry about that. Agatha Black had better table manners thàn me. Better even than Mum. If anything, she was too posh. It was only a fry-up. She sat ram-rod straight and after every mouthful dabbed her mouth with her hanky and kept smiling at the babies. The twins, who had calmed down, acted like they were bewitched by her.

"They like you, Randolph," Mum said. "I couldn't get them to settle ten minutes ago. Now look at them: good as gold."

I swallowed at the mention of gold and saw Agatha's eyes light up.

"So, where's Randolph from then?" Dad asked, pouring tea from the pot into his cup.

"Actually," I began, frantically trying to think of somewhere, "he's from... England. He's new around here." I felt like Pinocchio. If I was Pinocchio, my nose would be ten feet long by now.

"Well, that's a big place," Dad said, reaching for another slice of toast. "Where in England exactly?"

I racked my brains trying to think of places. I said the only place I could think of. "London," I blurted out.

Mum suddenly looked impressed. "The big city!" she said. "What brings Randolph to a wee place like Peebles after grand London town?"

"The country air," I said, wiping the tomato sauce on my plate with a crust of toast. I noticed Agatha copy me. "You see," I went on, in full flow now, "poor

Randolph's quite pale and small. His parents thought the hills of the Borders would make him healthier."

Mum seemed happy with that explanation because she smiled at Randolph who smiled back. Mum winked at me then got up from the table, saying how nappies needed changed and how us lads should have a fun time and how I was not to lead Randolph astray.

I was clearing the table when Agatha turned green and threw up Dad's fantastic fry-up all over the kitchen floor.

"I thought it was maybe a bit much for a wee guy like that," Dad said, while I groaned and Agatha found a cloth and wiped up the mess, with Dad's help.

Once the sick was cleaned up, Dad said fresh air would be a tonic and how about a snowball fight for me and Agatha grinned like she knew what a snowball fight was.

She did! Despite having thrown up, she got right into it and whacked me loads and was an even better aim than Dad. It occurred to me, seeing her running around, scooping up snow and hurling her snowballs through the air, that she was a tomboy. And maybe in 1812 it wasn't so easy for a girl to be tomboy? Maybe me and Agatha could stay pals and she could stay in the future for ever? She was better fun than Robbie and Will (Robbie, who at this very moment would be skating like a pro with a hot-dog in his hand in Edinburgh's Winter Wonderland...).

I tried not to think about Winter Wonderland. After we'd pelted each other with snow for ages, Agatha suddenly shouted out, "Let us make a snowman!"

Dad was in the middle of brushing snow off his jacket. He glanced up at Agatha, looking a bit bewildered that voiceless Randolph had suddenly recovered. "Let us make a snowman!" I yelled, trying to sound just like Agatha.

Dad scratched his head and looked from me to Agatha. Then he grinned and joined in. "Yeah, let us make a snowman!"

And that's what we did. Dad rolled the biggest bit for the body. I patted it smooth and Agatha rolled up the head. She lifted the round white ball and plonked it down on top of the body. Then we all ran around finding branches for arms, and pebbles for eyes, and I ran into the kitchen and found a carrot for a nose. Agatha carved lips into the face, and ran her fingers across the top of the head, giving the snowman hair. It was a great snowman. Agatha couldn't keep a huge smile off her face.

When we eventually went inside Dad made everyone hot chocolate, then, without warning, he picked up the remote control and flicked on the TV. Suddenly men were running across a football pitch chasing a ball and the crowd was cheering. Poor Agatha dropped her hot chocolate, screamed and turned pale.

As I gaped at the pool of brown liquid on the carpet, I thought maybe I would have to change some bits of the essay. Children from the past, though they are quite brave, would be scared by things we are used to, things that are fast or loud. Agatha, I was learning, was very scared of modern inventions. Cars made her scream. Fizzy juice made her sneeze. TV made her panic. The phone ringing made her jump out of her skin.

I looked from the puddle of hot chocolate, to her black-laced boots, then up to her pale face. She was still shivering with the shock of the TV and Dad, down on his hands and knees, was once again cleaning up after her. Agatha, her teeth chattering, couldn't peel her eyes away from the screen. I found the remote control and switched it off. She slumped back and seemed to relax after that. Then seeing my dad on his hands and knees she gasped, jumped up and helped him. So did I, mumbling how poor Randolph was not himself, tonsils and all that.

After the TV fiasco I took Agatha to my room and set about explaining life in the twenty-first century to her. I showed her the radiator, which, although it was painted white, was hot like a fire. She touched it, yelped and jumped backwards. I laughed and so did she. That's something I liked about her. She had a good sense of humour. I showed her my phone and flicked through photos, mostly of me, Robbie and Will making silly faces.

She looked discombobulated (I like that word). I told her so, thinking I would impress her. She just nodded and said if I was transported 200 years would not I also be feeling discombobulated? She peered at the phone, scratched her head and said, "But how does this work?"

"It's simple," I said, "you just click this button."

She shook her head. "No, Saul. But how does this little contraption make these likenesses?"

"Well… umm…" my voice trailed off. "It's chips," I answered, lamely.

She looked confused. "Chips?"

I shrugged. "It's like your dad's time travel. It's a mystery."

She touched the screen and winced. "It isna really you. It is like someone painted your likeness. And it has a bleak feel."

"It's called technology," I said, breezily, as though that explained everything. "We've got a lot of it." But Agatha shook her head, either still confused or not interested, I wasn't sure which.

"Ah, but we made a majestic man of snow," she cried as though she had suddenly remembered him. She ran to the window, peered out at the snowman then came back and flopped on the edge of my bed. She pressed her finger to her lips. That's what she did when she was thinking. Next thing a smile lit up her face. "Now, Saul, do you play chess?"

Well, I didn't, but I did have an old chess set, and for the next two hours Agatha taught me everything she knew about the game. I learnt how to move pawns, how to jump with the knight, how to defend the king and how to diagonally move the bishop. I never enjoyed a game so much. Until she jumped over my castle, took my queen, banged her queen down right in front of my king and declared: "Check mate!"

Even two hundred years ago, I wrote in my head, *children played the game of chess. It is a difficult game of strategy, which means clever planning.*

Agatha lifted my defeated king off the board, and shook my hand. I was getting quite used to the hand-shaking routine. "Thank you for an enjoyable game," she said, polite as ever. "Would you like to play a hand of cards now?"

I settled back on my beanbag. "Nah, know what I'd really like?"

"To hear more about 1812 perchance?"

13

"You got it Randolph," I said, making myself comfy, "more, once upon a time in 1812 your dad turned steam red and your monkey wore a jacket and…"

"And… in the house next door there dwells a boy who behaves extremely ill. His name is Dick and he likes nothing better than frightening poor Agatha Black half to death."

"Really?" I said. "You never mentioned him before."

"I make mention of Dick as little as possible. I fall into a bad humour simply thinking about him. But now that I am far away he canna find me. That is one consolation in being lost in the future. And of course making your acquaintance, Saul," she added quickly.

"Thanks, Agatha," I said, forgetting the Randolph disguise and feeling chuffed.

Agatha gave a little sigh. "Horrid Dick. He is my great tormentor. You see, his father is famed as a horseman and can outrun any rider. Dick is all made up about it and takes every opportunity to make fun of dear Father. And of course he pokes fun at me, and strikes me and mocks me. Oh, the devilish names he calls me dinna bear repeating."

Of course I immediately wanted to know what they

were. She flushed red and told me some of them – the not-so-awful ones I bet. "Cur! Half-baked tumshie! Eariwig! Daft muckle numpty! Milk curdler! Plague face!" She buried her face in her hands, sighed then said, "And as if name calling is not bad enough, he is aye trying to kiss me. Ugh! He says with a father out of his wits like my father is, and a mother cold in the grave, no gallant buck would ever take me for a wife. He is perfectly horrid, but the heart must needs be good and virtuous and so I mustna curse him. He is forever saying how females are of little use, and it is true, and it plagues me, but there it is."

"But you're not useless, you help your dad," I protested, suddenly hating this Dick as much as I hated Crow.

"But we females canna defend our country. Females canna join the Militia. This is what Dick means." She looked sadly at me. "Of course, I am willing to help Father. But regard me Saul. I am lost. Yet I am convinced Father is even now busy in his study, seeking to win me back to current time. And doubtless horrid Dick, to make matters worse, is pressing his podgy nose hard up against the window pane and pulling faces at Father. Oh, he squints like a bag of nails. Oh! When I dwell on my lost state, it is insufferable. I well know what vulgar Dick will say, when he gets wind of my disappearance."

"What?" I asked her, sitting forward and looking probably a bit too eager, "What will vulgar Dick say?"

"He will burst into the house without so much as a by-your-leave and he will put the fear of God into poor Father. The body snatchers got her, that's what he will say."

"The body snatchers?"

"Aye. Though it is more often the poor folk they prey on, the vagrants with no homes. And the scavengers and hawkers. The body snatchers kill them then sell their bodies to the doctors in Edinburgh to cut open and study inside. Three poor tinkers were lost from Peebles and everyone said it was the body snatchers got them."

I felt a lump in my throat. First hangings and now body snatchers? "Really?" I said, wimpishly.

"Indeed. And in addition a great many wicked sons of men are hanged for Highway robbery, housebreaking and murder."

I gulped. Agatha came from a dangerous time. She saw my worried face and smiled. "But I am a good and proper Christian and do say my prayers and read the Bible. The Lord is my shepherd and them who do ill and sin face eternal damnation but I wish only good."

I scratched my head, thought with a gulp about all my lies, and went off to find a pack of cards.

I think Mum and Dad were secretly pleased I had a new pal. And probably they thought somebody from London with manners like Randolph would be a good influence on me. Anyway, later that afternoon, after me and Agatha had played cards for ages and eaten ham sandwiches for lunch, Mum popped her head round the door, saying there was a holiday film on at the Eastgate Centre and did we want to go?

"Definitely," I said, jumping up and grabbing the money she was offering.

"Call it your Christmas treat," she said, "and if there's any left over buy Randolph some popcorn."

Ten minutes later, me and Agatha were heading out into the Peebles winter afternoon. I punched the air, I was that happy. I couldn't believe my luck. I had wanted to see this film for ages and now here I was, on my way to the cinema. Agatha, who was also looking pretty excited, was wearing my old jacket. "Is it a play we are going to see?" she asked me, practically skipping along the street, she was that excited. I told her it was kind of a play, but way better. I flipped my hood up and she did the same. Glancing at Agatha was like glancing into a mirror.

We turned into the slushy High Street just as the snow started to fall. Being out with Agatha was like being out with a two-year-old child. Every ten seconds there was something to stop and stare at: cars, buses, the way people were dressed. Now it was the Christmas lights strewn across the High Street. She pointed up to them and laughed. "Oh, how glorious," she cried. "Oh, see, Saul. They are like stars fallen into the town."

"Yeah," I mumbled, but I was getting kind of tired stopping all the time. I glanced up at the church clock. Twenty-five past three. The movie started at half past. "They're ok." I beckoned for her to get a move on. "But Robbie says they've got much better ones in

Edinburgh. Come on Randolph, if we're late we'll get rubbish seats."

She pulled herself away from gazing up at the lights and fell into step beside me; but not for long. Next thing I could hear her make funny whimpering noises, then I felt her tugging at my jacket. "What now?" I snapped, swinging round and scowling at her. She looked like she was going to throw up. Not again, I thought, feeling really annoyed. "Come on, Agatha," I said, "we don't want to be late."

"So very many shops and all burning so brightly. It jumps into me," she said, shielding her eyes, which I thought was going a bit far. And then a lorry chugged past. It was an old lorry and a dark cloud of exhaust smoke belched out. "Ah! I am overcome!" Agatha clamped her hands over her mouth. "The smell chokes me in my very throat," she cried in a muffled choking voice.

"Sorry about that," I said, as if it was my fault. I was feeling responsible for the whole of the twenty-first century: for the Christmas lights and the shops and the traffic and the exhaust fumes. "Oh, come on, Agatha. Listen, we don't want to be late." It was a big deal for Mum to give me enough cash for an afternoon out like this and I really wanted to see the film, and the adverts. I didn't want to miss a bit. I pulled off my scarf and shoved it in her hands. "Here, wrap that round your mouth, Miss Sensitive, and let's go!"

The scarf mask seemed to help. She stopped moaning and trotted along the High Street next to me. "When I am returned," she said, her voice still muffled, "the smells of the future are the first thing I will tell of. And then of the smells that are gone."

"Like what?" I asked, thinking if I got her talking about the past she might forget the bright lights and bad fumes of the present. "Bad drains?" By this time we were halfway along the High Street. I could see the neon lights of the cinema in the distance. I wanted to run faster but the pavement was slippy. "Or swine?"

"Sour fruit, peat smoke and, most of all, the horses and their dung. All are vanished. Ach Saul, some market days, when old meat turns in the sun I feel quite faint with the stench."

I tried to imagine where the market would be. Agatha did her mind reading thing again. "It is close by here," she said, slowing down and pointing to the Tontine Hotel in the middle of the High Street. "Or I think it is. So much is changed. Ah, Saul, what bustle market day brings." She pulled a face. "And there are always sinful folks to see locked in the stocks. Some have rotten eggs thrown into their dishonest faces. And there is always someone making music on the street. Pray, what is drains?"

"Things underground that stink," I said, imagining Crow locked in the stocks. We were about to pass the sweetie shop. I could smell the fudge. "Keep going, Randolph," I said. "Fast, and just keep your eyes on your feet." Of course she couldn't resist a peek.

"Confectionary," she cried out, chuffed she recognised something. She pulled down the scarf and pressed her face up against the glass of the shop window. I felt like a spoilsport yanking her away.

"Keep walking, Randolph," I insisted, steering her away from the shop and along the street. "You're doing just fine, and see when we get to the cinema, don't go on about the smells, ok?"

She nodded, but she was still oggling everything around her like her head was on a swivel: more Christmas lights, Santa hats on folk along the street, a woman's high heels and a man on the street corner playing the fiddle. "The cinema," I went on, heading for the entrance, "smells of toffee popcorn and confectionary!"

By this time we had reached the Eastgate. The glass doors slid open as we stood in front of them. Agatha jumped back and gasped. "Opened by a ghost," she whispered. I grabbed her by the arm and we were through, into the brightly lit foyer. "It smells burnt," she said, twitching her nose.

"Oh shut up, will you? This is supposed to be fun. This is a treat. If you're going to rant on about smells maybe you should just head back to the den. Jeez! I've been wanting to come to the cinema for ages and you're spoiling it."

She squeezed my arm. "Sorry."

I shuffled to the ticket counter. She shuffled beside me. "Yeah," I said, "just try and relax, ok?"

"Ok." She slipped her hand under my elbow.

I wriggled free and glared at her. "Hey, Randolph!"

She went red. She bit her lip. "Oh! I forget myself." She wrung her hands together then blinked, and kept blinking. "The light," she whispered, rubbing her eyes, "is extremely bright. It pierces me."

This wasn't going to work. To make matters worse, just at that moment rap music blared out of loud speakers. Agatha squealed and clamped her hands to her ears.

"Yes, son?" the woman at the ticket desk said. "What do you want?"

I looked at Agatha. I looked at the ticket woman. I could tell by the pitying way the woman smiled at me she thought Agatha had something wrong with her. Agatha was still whimpering in the middle of the foyer with her hands pressed over her ears. I looked down at the notes in my hand. "Nothing," I muttered.

"Well, don't hold the queue up, there's a good lad," she said, waving for me to get out the way.

I bought two huge packets of toffee popcorn and me and Agatha went for a walk along by the river instead. I got her away from the noise and the smells and the bright lights, and soon the only noise was of me and her chomping on popcorn. And the river that swished under us as we stood on the bridge.

"I am awfa sorry," she said.

"Yeah," I muttered, "no worries," and I stared down into the black water, wondering how I was going to get this girl back to where she came from. I still had two pounds left. I took 50p and threw it into the river.

"What are you doing?" she asked.

"Praying," I said.

She lowered her popcorn bag to the ground then wrapped her fingers together. "Therefore I," she said, closing her eyes, "shall pray too."

And that's what we did. I wished that I might manage to get her back to 1812. I wished for Mum not to ask too many questions about the film. And I wished for Albert Black to not get hanged for losing his daughter.

It felt like a long time we were praying, and wishing, with the river swishing under us. "Amen," she whispered.

"Amen," I said.

14

After I walked Agatha back to the den, I ran all the way home. I felt kinda miserable. I had £1.50 in my pocket, a bellyache from all that popcorn and I hadn't seen the film. As I hurried along the snowy road, so that I would have something to tell Mum, I started from the ads I'd seen for the film and made up a story about pirates and a sinking ship and a treasure chest filled with gold. And a boy who tried to save a beautiful girl but was made to walk the plank. It was so real I was starting to believe I had actually seen it.

Turning into our empty street, the boy in my imaginary film was down on his knees begging for his life, when I heard a real, horrible, gut-churning, evil laugh. "Hey, Sauly-boy. Where ya think ya goin'?"

I didn't look round. My house was only a minute away. Why had I walked on that side of the road? I gulped. I felt my palms sweat. I looked down and kept going. "Not got no money in ya pocket?" Crow was sitting on Sam's gate and I was going to have to walk right past. "A pound's fine. Call it protection money. Then you and me's brothers."

I made like I hadn't heard. I walked right on past, but my steps got faster and faster. The gate squeaked and next thing Crow cut in front of me. "Or fifty pence if ya poor," he hissed, so close I could smell his smoky breath. He grabbed my arm. I felt my legs turn to jelly. I fumbled in my pocket, felt for the 50p and gave it to him. "Got no more in there?" he whined, blocking my way. I clenched my fists. I wanted to punch him. I wanted to scream and tell him to leave me alone. I tightened my fingers around the pound coin. "Hand it over, nerd." He laughed his horrible empty laugh. My heart was racing. "I don't like waiting, ya hear?"

"I haven't got any more," I said, my voice all high and frightened.

"Liar," he hissed, then he pushed me. I stumbled back but didn't fall. He pulled my hand out of my pocket. It was still clenched around the pound coin. Just then a car slowed down and stopped on the road. "I'll get you next time," he said, moving away. I heard his footsteps fade up the street. The car window slid down.

"You alright, laddie?" It was big Mr Drummond from round the corner. I nodded then bolted over the road and pushed the garden gate open. My heart was pounding as I dashed up the path and into the house.

"Mum!" I shouted, as I stood panting in the hallway.

"I'm giving the twins a bath," she called out. "I hope the film was fun."

"Yeah," I said, dropping my jacket onto the carpet. I went into the kitchen, poured myself a glass of milk and flopped down on the sofa. The telly was on but I switched it off. I went back to the bit in my head where the boy on the pirate ship was begging for his life. He jumped to his feet, broke the bands tied round his hands, tore off his blindfold and *roared*. The pirates screamed. They turned on their heels. The boy ran after them. They were terrified of him and they jumped overboard. Then the boy untied the girl. "You're free now," he said, and they got the treasure and the ship.

By the time Mum appeared from settling the twins, which wasn't for ages, I felt like I'd seen a really good film. "Randolph seems like a nice boy," she said, as she headed for the kitchen. "Fancy cheese on toast?"

I shook my head.

"Well, I do." She propped the door open so she could chat to me. "Yes, a polite boy, but a bit troubled looking. London's no place for a child. Good thing he's in Peebles. It'll put colour in his cheeks."

I got up from the sofa. The last thing I needed was an interrogation about Randolph. "Mum?" I said, hovering between the kitchen and the living room. "Can I go on the computer?"

"What for?" The cheese on toast was bubbling under the grill. It smelt good.

"Um, the history essay. I need to find out stuff."

I watched Mum fetch a plate from the cupboard. She slid her snack onto it. "For half an hour. Not a minute more." Then she took a big bite. "Delicious. Sure you don't want some?"

I shook my head and dashed over to the desk in the living room.

"Well, don't go getting lost in the past," she said.

Of course I didn't Google the word history. I checked

over my shoulder to make sure Mum was safely in the kitchen, then I typed in the words

SEARCH: | time travel |

There were 250,000,000 hits. That's a lot! Millions of people and clubs and secret societies and weirdo groups had loads to say about time travel. The first thing that flashed up was a red advert for travelling clocks. **TAKE IT WITH YOU ON HOLIDAY** it said. "No thanks," I mumbled, clicking and clicking. I couldn't believe the number of sites trying to sell time travel machines. There was one with a picture of a Tardis-style telephone box in space. What a joke! **Only £65,000** it said. You could buy time-travel t-shirts. There was even a recipe for time-travel chocolate cake. My head throbbed.

I glanced at the clock in the corner of the screen. I only had ten more minutes. I clicked on Professor Stephen Hawking. His site had little drawings of wormholes in spacetime. He said if we could only work out how to get down these wormholes, we could time travel. Somehow, I didn't think that was going to work for Agatha!

I could hear Mum clattering away with the dishes. She was whistling and the kettle was boiling. I needed to narrow things down a bit, so I keyed in

SEARCH: | time travel Peebles |

That narrowed it down loads. Only one thing came up, which was a scan from some big library collection of a boring-looking old fashioned letter.

From George Macrimmon,

it said at the top,

Peebles, Scottish Borders, 1953.

What people do not understand is that transportation through time is in fact achievable.

I wished I was faster at reading. I could hear Mum making tea. She'd be through soon.

Travelling through time is a science not new to the men of Peebles. Few now remember these early inventors and bold souls. Yet research handed down through many generations shows that to travel through time is not dependent upon outer para...

something or other. I scrolled down fast, trying hard to understand the words.

The method requires unpara...

something

...concentration and purity of intention. The mind free of clamour focuses on the intended voyage. The purified heart opens, pouring love and will on the time and the place to be visited. And the body knows without a grain of doubt that success in the voyage will prevail. Thus the traveller of pure body, mind and soul unites fully to the purpose and hears the echo of times past. And follows it.

So very simple,

the letter said at the end,

yet almost impossible.

I read the letter four times and tried to memorise it. The more I read, the simpler it seemed. If you really want to time travel, you can. At least that's what I made of it. "Two minutes, Saul," Mum called from the kitchen.

I felt exhausted. Quickly, I typed in

SEARCH: | gold Peebles |

CASH FOR YOUR UNWANTED GOLD

flashed up on the screen.

TILLY'S PAWN SHOP, 79 NORTHGATE, PEEBLES.

"Right, Saul, turn it off now."

I memorised the address. Then I turned the computer off, and thought about George Macrimmon and how the heart had to fully unite with the intended voyage.

I could turn off the computer but I couldn't turn off the shiver that kept running up and down my spine. It was still tingling there later when I tried to get to sleep.

Waking up the next morning, I immediately scribbled down the words that I remembered:

The mind focuses. The heart opens. The body knows.

"It's breakfast time," Mum called through from the kitchen. I rolled the scrap of paper into a scroll and put it in my rucksack.

15

There wasn't time to go to the den before school but I was planning on nipping out at lunchtime and using my leftover £1 to buy Agatha a ham roll. She'd told me she loved them.

The pavements were slushy and all the hills around Peebles were white. As I walked to school, breathing in the chilly morning air, I felt excited. I'd found a way to help Agatha get back home to 1812. And as far as the history prize went, maybe I had already learned enough. So much had been going on I didn't know whether I'd actually ever really get round to writing the essay. I dandered a bit, thinking about stuff. School was ok. Not that I was top of the class or anything like that. Bottom more like. But break was good, and football, and basketball, and storytelling. Me, Robbie and Will sat at the back in class having a laugh, but hopefully not annoying Mrs Veitch so often that we ended up getting into trouble. The swots sat at the front, always sticking up their hands to answer every question. I never did. I gave that up in Primary 2. Actually, perhaps it'd be best not to do that essay. If I handed in something extra like that, it'd give Mrs Veitch the shock of her life.

The absolute best thing about school is the big hill at the back. It's great for bikes, and Robbie did a really high jump using it as a ramp. So did Will, but then he went and fell and hurt himself, so the school banned the hill. But me and Will and Robbie still go.

Anyway, that Monday morning, I decided that if Agatha was going to zoom back to history any day now, I should at least let her have a day in a school of the future. She'd told me girls hardly ever went to school in 1812 and not that many boys went either. When I asked her how come she knew so much stuff, she said when her mum was alive and the family had a bit more money she'd had a governess who taught her reading and handwriting and numbers at home.

Other kids at my school had brought visitors before. Will once brought his cousin who was over from South Africa. He was called Merl and he sat between me and Will and drew a giraffe. I didn't know whether you could just turn up with your visitor, or whether you had to get a note about it or something?

When I got to school, I could tell Robbie was itching to tell me all about Winter Wonderland, but I didn't ask. I pretended I had forgotten he even went there. He looked a bit miffed, especially when I started talking to Will.

I told Will how Randolph wanted to come to school, and Will said it was allowed but you did have to get a letter from your parents. It was Will's idea to make Randolph my cousin. At break I went on the computer and typed one up. I kept it short.

Dear teachers

Saul's cousin is on a visit from London. He is called Randolph. Could he visit the school for a day please on Tuesday?

Thank you
Mrs Martin

It looked fine, except I wished I had made Randolph come from somewhere else, like Outer Mongolia or Romania. Mr Bradley, the deputy head, came from London. He might ask Randolph questions about it – then we'd be stumped! Anyway, I handed the letter in at the office, and that lunchtime ran to the den to tell Agatha all about it.

Except when I got there, Agatha was busy playing flap the fish. "I cut one for you," she cried out as I burst into the den. There was Miss Agatha Black, down on her hands and knees, banging the palm of her hand on the wooden floor to make a paper fish jerk forward. "Then we can race," she said, "which is by far the best fun. Here Saul," she beckoned for me to kneel down beside her. "This is your fish. Bang hard, but you may not touch it, ok?"

"Ok, Agatha!" I flung down my rucksack, yanked off my gloves and lined up my fish. Then we were off. What a racket. Agatha had obviously put in a lot of practice. She managed to make her fish flap like a wild thing. My fish just bumped up and down really slowly. "I win!" she yelled, then we did the hand-shaking thing.

Then I told her about school.

She was so excited she ran out of the den and danced about the garden. Then she practised speaking like me. We were so carried away about the school visit that I almost forgot the scrolled up paper I had in my rucksack. Agatha was sitting on the fallen tree trunk, tucking into her ham roll when I fished it out of my bag. "I think I know how to get you back home," I said.

She gulped on her ham roll and gazed up at me. "What?"

"Remember how I told you about technology? Well, we've got this thing called the internet. You can find out about everything. So I found out about time travel." I was leaning back against a tree, slowly un-rolling the paper. "The mind focuses. The heart opens. The body knows." I looked at her and smiled. "It's simple," I said, not mentioning the impossible bit. "What it means," I went on, feeling like I was Mr Macrimmon, "is that basically you have to really want to travel back through time. You have to love it, and you have to totally trust with every bit of you that it's going to happen. At least, I think that's what it means."

"Have faith, you mean?"

"Yeah, something like that." I handed her the paper. "So, maybe if I can get all the other stuff, we can try it in a couple of days?"

"The gold also?" She stared at me, her blue eyes like huge pools.

I shrugged. I had been so excited about Macrimmon's plan I had forgotten about Agatha's obsession with gold. In the distance I heard the church bells. I had to go soon. "I haven't figured that bit out yet."

Agatha's face fell and the scroll dropped from her grasp. "Then it willna work."

"But this man says if you totally believe, it will work. Agatha, he was from Peebles, this professor man," I said, as if that made it all ok.

"As was Mister Albert Black, may I remind yea." She gazed glumly down at the sheet of paper.

"Agatha, listen. I know you're lost and all that, but Mister Albert Black did manage to put you into the future. I mean, let's face it, that is pretty incredible."

Agatha didn't look too impressed.

"And you know," I went on, "the letter didn't mention Albert Black exactly, but it kind of did."

She eyed me quizzically.

"Yeah," I said, trying to sound cheery, "it said men in Peebles had been working on time travel for a long time. I'm pretty sure they meant Albert Black. I think he is a bit famous."

"Really?"

"Really."

She chewed her lip. After a while she smiled up at me. "Saul, I am heartened indeed, yet I will feel better by far when we have proper gold. With faith and gold I will surely return home." Then she made an effort to cheer up. "But in the meantime," she grinned, "I am so very merry to be a schoolgirl. It will indeed give me majestic pleasure!"

"Good!" I scooted up the garden and into the den to grab my gloves and head back to school.

Agatha ran after me, eager to show me what she'd been up to. She spread paper out on the floor.

"Afore yea hasten away, pray look," she said, her face flushed and her eyes shining. She was so excited about showing me her drawings she seemed to have forgotten all about the lack of gold. She fell to her knees and pointed. "Here I have tried to make the pretty Christmas lights." She gave me two seconds to look at that one, then pointed to another one. "And here the magic cinema doors." She had loads of drawings of really ordinary stuff. But they were terrific. I was seriously impressed. "See here, Saul, this one is of the large roaring carriage."

"That's a lorry," I told her, giving her the thumbs-up approval. Though Agatha Black had never seen lorries till a few days ago, her drawing of one was bang on.

"And this is the striped boilings in the glass jar."

"Looks like sweeties to me."

"Sweeties," she repeated, licking her lips like she was tasting the word. "Now, pray, close your eyes." I did but then I peeked, so she found her handkerchief and tied it round my head, over my eyes. I heard her fumble with a sheet of paper and wondered what was coming next. "And now, you may look!" She pulled off my blindfold.

"Jeez! That's me!" There I was on the floor, staring back up at me. Weird!

"Do you like it? I did take many hours over this."

"Wow! It's good. I mean, Agatha, you're a great artist. It's like I'm looking into a mirror."

She blushed and shook her head. "'Tis a pastime,

nothing more." Then she folded up the drawing of me and slid it and the handkerchief under her dress and flouncy hat.

I really had to go. Quickly, I gave her the rest of the food I'd managed to sneak out of the house, and told her I'd see her at half past eight the next morning, outside the launderette. I wittered on about how I was sorry but I had basketball after school, then after that Mum wanted me to help her with the twins, and then...

"Dinna worry about me, Saul," Agatha said. "I am right content here. I have much to draw, and much to think on, and am now so very at sixes and sevens about school. I will need to spend hours practising my speaking, and all manner of things. I will be as busy as a little bee, and it will be the morning before I know it. And besides, your sleeping-sack is warmer than my blanket at home." She waved to me as I slung the rucksack onto my back. "I am here but a short time," she said, smiling at me, "I must savour each moment."

16

"Hiya, Saul." Agatha was standing outside the launderette next morning, hoping from foot to foot – with excitement or cold, I couldn't tell. "Are you doing ok?"

"Never been better," I lied, but I was impressed with her speaking. It sounded like she'd been practising all night.

She skipped over to me. "Oh, I am that awfa much in a spin about school," she said.

I started walking down the street and she fell into step beside me. "Me too, Randolph," then after a moment I added, "Umm, don't say much, ok? And don't gaze around all the time, pop-eyed, like you just landed on the planet."

"Sure," she said, giggling, "I will do as you do."

I laughed. It came out sounding all nervous. I walked fast and Agatha slithered about in the snow trying to keep up. I wanted us to get to school early, and slip into the building before everybody else. "You're my cousin, remember?"

"Sure," she said, again.

"Your name's Randolph. You're from London. You haven't been too well, and you're in Peebles to get better. And you've had tonsillitis and your throat is sore. Got that?"

Agatha nodded and flashed me her brightest smile. She looked really healthy. "And don't smile so much."

She frowned. "Pray I never catch the measles. Little Bessie from next door died of the measles. There isna an epidemic in the school, is there, Saul?"

I laughed, though it wasn't funny. "Nobody dies of measles now," I said, and we went through the big iron gates into the cemetery. I usually cut through the cemetery to get to school. It's the fastest way. But now I got the creepiest feeling as we hurried past all these old gravestones. I imagined Bessie in a little white coffin, dead with the measles. "Come on, Randolph," I said, and ran the rest of the way.

When we reached the playground there was hardly anybody about. So far, so good. Agatha asked if she could look around and I said she could, if she was quick about it, before folk arrived. She gazed down at the hopscotch markings on the path. "I know this," she squealed. "We have this too." Before I could stop her she jumped and hopped up the squares. Then she stared in wonder at the massive wooden climbing frame. "May I?" she asked. I shrugged and off she went, like a soldier clambering over the ropes and wooden slats.

Then I waved for her to come back. Kids were beginning to stream into the playground and I wanted Randolph to attract as little attention as possible. Next thing we were standing in front of the school building. I wished Kingsland was old fashioned but it wasn't. I wished it had proper old-fashioned doors that couldn't swing open by themselves. Ghost doors, Agatha called this kind. And I wished the bell didn't screech. I gave Agatha a pair of Mum's wax ear-plugs I'd found in the bathroom cupboard. She shoved them in her ears – just in time because the bell screeched like a fire alarm. When we stood in the corridor taking our jackets off, Agatha leant over and winked at me. "I willna let yea down," she said.

"Ah! Your cousin I take it, Saul." Mrs Veitch strode up to Agatha who stuck out her hand. The teacher paused for a second, then smiled and pumped Agatha's hand up and down. "Now that's what I like in a boy: manners. And while you are visiting us, Randolph, perhaps you might teach Saul here a few." Then she strode off. Agatha winked at me again and we followed Mrs Veitch to the classroom.

I ran to get a spare seat and wedged it in next to my desk. I gestured for Agatha to sit down and what was so funny about that I don't know, but Robbie got a fit of the giggles. I glowered at him and he shut up. Then it was writing time.

Mrs Veitch gave us half an hour to write a story. The week before in school we had all watched a film about animals. Now we were to write about a day in the life of an animal. I chose a guinea pig but hardly wrote anything. I was too busy looking at what Agatha was writing. Actually, it was more her handwriting that got me. It was all loops and hoops. It was a dead giveaway. I scribbled at the bottom of my guinea pig story,
don't write so fancy
and pushed it over to her. She blushed.

"What are you up to, Saul?" the teacher said. She's got eyes like a hawk.

"Nothing," I mumbled. That's what I always say: "Nothing." Not: "Actually, Mrs Veitch, I'm telling Agatha here to pretend she's a boy. And to pretend she comes from London and not 1812 and to stop showing off her handwriting skills."

"Well, let Randolph do his best."

I did, and as far as I could make out, Randolph wrote about how monkeys like dressing up, just like we do! And she knows of one with the name of Pug who does wear a red waistcoat and loves everyone to watch him!

We made it to break and nothing bad had happened. Robbie and Will were building a snowman and shouted for us to join in. I could tell Robbie was still itching to spill the beans about his trip to Edinburgh. By this point I was feeling pretty torn between all my pals. "Come on, Randolph," I said, tugging at her arm, "let's make snow monkeys with Will and Robbie." Agatha laughed. I think she was really enjoying being at school, but she shook her head. She didn't want to make a snow monkey. Instead she kept staring at a shy girl from our class who was hunched over a book across in the bike shed.

"Who is she?" Agatha asked.

I shrugged. "Dunno, Nessa or something like that. She's got lice. And she never joins in with stuff." I'd never talked to Nessa or given her much thought. She never spoke in class or put her hand up. Will says she's really clever. But she's a weirdo. She's got no friends. It was Robbie who'd told me she had lice. And Will also said that her mum is dead.

"She looks nice," Agatha pulled away from me and ran over the snowy playground to where the girl who's always left out was reading.

"Hey, Randolph!" I shouted. "Come back." But she didn't, so I ran after her. "I said *lice*, not nice," I muttered under my breath.

By the time I got to the bike shed, Agatha had gone right up to the uncool girl. "Hello," Agatha said, "what is your name?"

"Hey, Randolph," I said, feeling stupid, "come on." I flashed a look at the girl, who lowered her book and peered over the top of it. You could hardly see her eyes for all the greasy hair hanging down over her face.

"Agnes," she said, then hid behind her book again. I wondered how Agatha could think this girl looked nice when you couldn't even see her.

"Randolph," I said, sharper this time. "Let's go."

"It is a pleasure to meet you, Agnes," Agatha said.

I felt like a major fool standing next to the girl nobody ever goes near. I thought about all the stories of lice and incurable diseases. I shifted back a step. But not Agatha – she stepped forward and was getting ready for the hand-shaking routine. To my total shock the shy girl smiled and shook Agatha's hand.

"My name," said Agatha, smiling broadly at her new chum, "is…"

"Randolph," I cut in, fast. "He's my cousin. He's from London. Right then, Randolph. We have to go."

But it was like I didn't exist. These two weird girls just gazed at each other and went on shaking hands. I glanced from one to the other. They had the same coppery hair, except of course Agatha's was now short and the uncool girl's was all over her face. But then she shook her hair back and I could see her little upturned nose, quite like Agatha's.

"Look!" I butted in. Will and Robbie had given up on the snowman and they were charging up the playground towards us. "Come on, Randolph, the bell's going to go. We need to get back."

I dragged Agatha away, but she kept gazing over her shoulder at the girl. "How lovely she is," she murmured. "What a glorious thing today to make acquaintance with Agnes. When is the next break?"

"Never," I muttered. Just then Will or Robbie threw a snowball and it landed on my back. I swung round, scooped up snow and hurled a snowball back. It hit Robbie hard on the arm.

"Ouch!" he yelled. "That hurt."

Then the school bell rang. Agatha's stupid pink ear-plugs must have fallen out. She flung her hands to her ears and screamed. Then she grabbed at me. "It's ok, Agatha," I said, forgetting all about Randolph. "It's only the bell. It just means the end of break."

"The end?" Her face was white as the snow.

"Well, for now," I mumbled. Everyone gaped at us as

they filed into the school building – especially Robbie, making a big show of rubbing his arm and looking wounded.

I steered the trembling Agatha into the corridor. I didn't know how much more of this I could take. Just then, Agnes, the left out girl, passed us. She stopped and put a hand on Agatha's trembling shoulder. "It's just a silly bell," she said, and instantly Agatha calmed down.

17

Agatha might have calmed down but not me. I was a jumping bag of nerves. No way could I handle a whole school day of this. During French I planned our escape. I would say I was going to show Randolph where the toilets were, then zoom, out we'd go, back to the peace and safety of the den.

Agatha, though, was looking rapt. She gazed at the teacher like she was in love with her and I watched her repeat the words: *jaune, blue, noir, rouge*... She must have felt my eyes on her. She turned round and beamed at me. *Verte, blanche, rose*...

"Randolph is giving me far more attention than you are, Saul," Mrs Veitch said, striding down the aisle and glaring at me. "What is red?"

"Rose?" I said, thinking how the Valentine card I got from Mum said roses are red.

"Wrong," she said, then swung round and smiled at Randolph. "You tell your cousin, Randolph."

"*Rouge*," replied Agatha, so pleased with herself I was scared she was going to jump up and down.

"Bravo," said Mrs Veitch and strutted off. Her high heels went snap, snap, snap and my fingers on the desk went tap, tap, tap. The teacher stopped before she reached her desk, swung round, stared at me and said, "Stop that irritating noise."

I couldn't very well ask to go to the toilet now. So I sat glumly through French while Agatha hung on the teacher's every word. I doodled on my jotter. It looked like a pirate jumping into the sea. I looked up when the teacher said, "Who can tell me where they live – in French?" She scanned the sea of faces and just when it looked like no one would, Nessa Nobody put up her hand. You could hear this little gasp of surprise ripple round the classroom. Agnes never ever put up her hand. Mrs Veitch looked as surprised as the rest of us. "Ah, right then." I could see her brain scrabbling around trying to remember Agnes's name. "Right, *jeune fille*," she said (whatever that means), "what is it?"

"*J'habite à Peebles. C'est une petite ville au sud d'Edimbourg*," Agnes said, sounding really French. "*En Ecosse*," she added, then blushed and looked down at her desk.

I think Mrs Veitch got a bit more than she bargained for. Robbie started to snigger. Mrs Veitch glared at him. "Bravo," shouted Agatha, quickly followed by Mrs Veitch. Then we all joined in. "Bravo! Bravo! Bravo!" until poor Agnes got up and ran out of the room. Agatha ran after her. It took Mrs Veitch ages to regain control of the class. I don't think she even noticed Agatha had gone. She fumbled around on her desk, pulled out the register, and I bet you anything she was looking for Agnes's name. Then, looking all flustered she whipped out a reading book, sat on the edge of her desk and read to us. When she paused to blow her nose, I asked if I could go to the toilet.

Course, I didn't go to the toilet. I dashed out into the playground. I looked on the climbing frame. I looked round by the bike shed. I even went up the hill behind the school. But Agatha and Agnes were nowhere to be seen. Down in the school I heard the bell screech for lunchtime. I could hear the church bells in the town centre strike midday. Suddenly I had a pretty good idea where Agatha and Agnes would be.

And I don't know why, but I didn't go after them. Maybe I thought I'd feel left out. Maybe I didn't want to catch lice. Or maybe I hadn't hung out with Robbie and Will for a while and I was starting to miss them. I went back into school and found them in the canteen. They waved me over and I slipped onto the bench beside them. Robbie was tucking into Scotch pie and beans. Will had a burger and salad.

"What you having?" Robbie said, shovelling another forkful of beans into his mouth.

"Nothing," I said. "Not hungry."

"And what about Harry Potter?" Will said. "Where's he gone?"

It took me a moment to figure out what he was going on about. "Oh, Randolph?"

They both nodded, and winked, and nudged me in the ribs. "Yeah. Like, your *cousin?*"

"He doesn't need me all the time," I said. "He's doing his own thing." But of course I couldn't help wondering what Agatha Black was doing and why she was suddenly all pally with Agnes. I shrugged and tried to forget about her.

"Anyway, Winter Wonderland was ace," Robbie said, leaning forward like it was a big secret. "The best ever. Oh man, you should have seen the big wheel. And I went on this ghost train, twice. Talk about scared. And I skated like a speed skater. Didn't fall once."

"Good for you," I mumbled.

"Shame you've never been," he said, shlurping back orange juice. Then he fumbled in his rucksack, pulled something out and shoved it behind his back. "Saul, I bought you a present. They've got this, like, market there. It's cool. And I got you this. Ta-da!" Then he made a big show of presenting me with a Rasta hat. He threw it at me like he was throwing a frisbee. I liked the hat. It was cool, all black and orange and red and green, and probably cost loads, but I threw it back in his face.

"Saul Martin," the dinner lady yelled at me. "That was uncalled for and ungrateful. I'm going to tell Mrs Veitch. You can wipe all the tables for that. Honestly!"

I hung my head.

"That wasn't nice," Will said.

"No," Robbie stuffed the Rasta hat back into his bag, "it wasn't nice at all." I didn't say a word. Robbie wasn't done, though. "Just cause you got these two babies crying all night long, you don't need to take it out on us." He leant in closer. "And like, who is this Randolph anyway? And what was he doing speaking to Nobody Nessa?" But he didn't wait for an answer. He sniffed, pushed back the bench, got up and marched off. Will followed him.

I never felt so miserable in my life. I wiped the tables and tried to stop the hot tears that welled up behind my eyes. Once the tables were done, I ran to the toilets and splashed cold water on my face. Then for the rest of the afternoon, I didn't say a word. In art I spent ages designing a Christmas card. I drew a Christmas tree and beside it I drew a monkey in a red jacket. I gave the monkey a pipe to smoke. But I rubbed out the pipe when the art teacher headed in my direction.

"What a cute thing," the art teacher said. "A monkey in a house."

And I wished Agatha was there, because she would have loved art. When the art teacher moved on to somebody else, I opened the card and scrawled across the top

To Agatha and Pug, from Saul, Peebles 2012.

Then I quickly stuffed it into my bag.

At the school gates, Robbie was obviously waiting for an apology. Or a fight. Having Crow after me was bad enough. I didn't need more enemies. Will was standing next to him. It was Will who spoke first. "Are we still in the gang?" he asked. I looked from Will to Robbie, then back to Will. They were both eyeing me like they didn't trust me anymore.

"Sure," I said, "we're having a break, right?" Then I looked at Robbie. "But I don't need your charity, ok? The hat was cool. But you don't need to feel sorry for me."

"It was just a present," he said. We stared at each other. He gave me a half smile. I gave him a half smile back.

"Yeah, well." I didn't know what else to say. I wanted to go to the den and find Agatha. I wanted to give her the Christmas card. But Will and Robbie were in the gang. It was their den too. And suddenly I was sick of all the lying and pretending. "Wanna come to Pisa?" I asked them.

"Sure," they both said.

"Wanna wear a cool hat?" said Robbie.

"Sure," I said, then we all fell about and did a bit of wrestling in the snow, and we laughed and I couldn't believe that I could feel so good after feeling so bad. Robbie shoved the Rasta hat on my head and we all pelted down the school path, along the cuddy and over the wasteland, yelling and cheering like idiots.

18

Halfway through the hedge we stopped. The sound of laughter was coming from the garden.

"No way do I want to get lice," Robbie said. "It's one thing Randolph being in the gang – for a few days – but Nessa Nobody is definitely not joining. If she does, I'm out."

"Me too," Will whispered.

"No fear," I hissed. "We're just going to check on Randolph. Give him a ham roll and a can of juice, then we'll tell Nessa to hop it."

"Agnes, you mean," whispered Will.

I led the way. We squirmed through the hedge and burst out into the garden like we were commandos. There was no sign of Agatha and Agnes. But I could hear them.

"Bet they're hiding from us," Robbie said, then he bolted away, ran up the garden and into the den. Will and me ran after him, my heart thumping. "They're not here," Robbie announced as we stumbled in. He whistled and looked about. "Pisa looks different. Randolph's done it up nice." Then he saw all the drawings. They were lined up across the floor like an exhibition. "Cool!" He looked at me. "Runaway Randolph do that?"

"Hm-mm," I mumbled.

Will was by his side and the two of them were having a right good stare. "Funny things to draw though," Will said. "I mean, whoever heard of anybody drawing a door handle? Or a light bulb? Or a lamp-post?"

"Yeah," Robbie laughed, "or a bit of popcorn? Definitely odd."

"Check out this one," Will said, "it's the doors at the Eastgate! And what's all this stuff?"

I stared at the pile of things in the corner that Will was pointing at. Agatha had been busy. There was a heap of earth on the floor, and water in Robbie's blue bowl. Beside the bowl there was a pile of small stones and a few shards of broken glass. Seems going home was always on her mind.

"Junk," I replied, waving my hand dismissively. Just at that moment another burst of laughter rang out from down the garden somewhere. "Anyway," I headed for the door, "I'm off to find them."

The laughter was coming from the other end of the garden. Me, Will and Robbie never went there. It was too overgrown and dangerous. But that's obviously where Agatha and her new pal were. I ran through the snow and stopped closer to the laughter. "Randolph!" I shouted.

Will and Robbie were a few steps behind. "Randolph!" we all shouted. "Where are you?"

Silence. I glanced round at my gang and shrugged.

"Tell him to quit mucking about," Robbie hissed.

"Randolph!" I shouted again, "Quit mucking about. Come on, where are you hiding?"

I heard rustling above me in a large tree. At the same time, a shower of snow floated down. I looked up. Something was moving. I couldn't believe it. I heard giggling from way above me. They were in that high tree!

Either Agatha or Agnes did a really good impression of an owl. "Randolph and Agnes are up there!" Will said, well impressed, and he hooted back.

The branches rustled and another dusting of snow fell down on us. They were like two monkeys. Then I recognised a black lace-up boot hovering in the air, and I saw it find a branch. "Stand back," Agatha called. Robbie whistled. Will gasped. The branch creaked, and she jumped down. She landed in the snow, rolled over, then sat up and beamed at us. Agnes did the same. Me and my gang just stared with our jaws hanging open as Agatha and Agnes, sitting on the ground, brushed the snow off their knees and laughed.

"Wow!" gasped Will, "that was so cool. Like, how did you manage to get up there? It's, like, *seriously* high!"

The girls laughed again, then Agatha pointed to Agnes and said, "She showed me how."

"What a… great place… to play," Agnes said, all breathless. "It's like a secret." She swept her eyes over the garden, and the den. "I didn't know."

"But now you do," said Agatha, clapping her hands.

"Yeah, but," said Robbie, all snappy, suddenly acting like he was the gang leader and not me, "this place is our secret. It's for *our* gang." He glared at Agnes.

"Yeah," said Will, pushing his shoulders back. "He's right."

"Yeah," I said, "and I'm the gang leader." I looked at the uncool girl sitting in the snow, not looking a bit uncool. Her hair was off her face for once. Her eyes shone and she didn't appear to have an incurable disease. She looked at me and I got the feeling she knew I was stumped for words. She jumped to her feet, brushed the snow off her school trousers and shook her hair down in front of her face.

"No problem," she said, "I'm leaving," and she rushed past us and disappeared through the hole in the hedge.

"Don't you dare tell anyone about this place," Robbie shouted after her, but I doubt she heard.

Agatha scrambled to her feet. Her face was glowing pink. "Lo! What glorious amusement!" she cried.

Robbie and Will looked at me, then at Agatha, then back at me.

"That's great, Randolph," I said. "So, anyway, *Randolph*," I made a big deal out of the name, "we just came to check you were ok."

Agatha clapped her hands together, beamed a huge smile at us and said, "Majestic!"

19

It was getting dark. What with all the business of the girls in the tree, we hadn't really noticed the light going. Mrs Veitch had been going on at school about how this week would end with the winter solstice, the shortest, darkest day of the year. Today's short afternoon was definitely over. The colour had drained away from the garden and we were like shadows standing in the snow. Even the moon was out.

"Right then," Will piped up, looking scared and glancing over his shoulder. "I have to go."

And it wasn't only because it was getting dark. I could see how uneasy they felt around Agatha. This Randolph disguise wasn't working. Agatha had completely forgotten how to speak, and she didn't really look like a boy at all. I decided to tell Will and Robbie everything. I was sick of lying. It was like I didn't even know what was true or not anymore. I just needed to spill the beans, then we'd be a gang like we used to be, with no secrets, and maybe they could help me get Agatha back where she belonged.

"Yeah, I have to go too," Robbie said. He grabbed me by the arm. "You coming, Saul?"

"Yeah," I said, "I've just got some stuff for Randolph.

Some food and that. I'll put it in the den. Then I'll catch you up." And they left, like they were in a massive hurry.

I went into the den and Agatha followed me. "Agnes is a girl to befriend, Saul," she said. "She isna like a demure lady. Not a whit. She is a marvel." She set about rubbing stones together. I watched sparks fly off them. They caught a twisted piece of gardening magazine and a tiny flame burned. "We have much in common. Like me, alas, her dear mother is in heaven." Agatha got down on her hands and knees and gently blew the flame. The flame grew and lit a twig. She sat back on her heels and looked up at me. "And like me, her hapless father does his best but struggles to put a loaf of bread upon the table. Did you note how threadbare her garments are?"

"Oh," was about all I could say. I was just getting used to the uncool girl having a name. "Poor Agnes." At that moment my phone beeped. "Text," I explained to Agatha, whipping out my phone. She peered over my shoulder, curious. I didn't recognise the number. And when I flicked open the text message I felt sick.

"What is it, Saul?" she asked, pressing her nose two inches away from the screen. "You have gone pale."

"Nothing," I said, snapping it shut. I felt my pulse race. I shoved the phone in my pocket, the text message blazing in my brain.

I'm after you. Crow

My mind raced. How did he get my number? I felt

well spooked at the idea of getting home alone in the dark. Mind-reader Agatha must have picked it up.

"Give no care to the horrid Dicks of this world," she said. "You are good and brave." Then she squeezed her hand over my arm. I shrugged her off and busied myself rummaging in my bag, trying to forget Crow and the text message.

I didn't have much to leave for her. I was sure I'd lost weight since meeting Agatha: I was giving her half my food. There were a couple of ham sandwiches and two packets of crisps, then I handed her the Christmas card. "It's for you and Pug," I said, a bit embarrassed after seeing what a good drawer she was.

"Mercy!" She held the picture close to the light of the fire and studied it. "I shall treasure this picture always," she said, then peered more closely. "It is a strange matter indeed to have a tree in a house."

"My teacher said the same about the monkey."

Agatha laughed and kissed the monkey on the card. From the distance I heard Robbie and Will shout, "Come on, Saul!" I felt relieved that they were nearby.

"Go!" she said, "pray, hasten to your friends. I am perfectly well."

"Tomorrow," I said, backing out of the den, "we could do something fun. Like, sledging or something? You know, going down a hill on the snow."

Agatha smiled at me. "I know of sledging," she said. "Now go!" Then she ran to the door of the den to wave to me. "Saul," she called just before I darted into the hole in the hedge. I turned back and looked at her. "Worry not," she said, smiling.

I grinned at her and disappeared into the hedge. Halfway through, I stopped and turned my phone off, promising myself not to turn it back on. I felt better then. I took a couple of deep breaths and reminded myself that I was the gang leader. And that I had been chosen to help Agatha Black and that was enough to worry about. And that I was going to write a history essay. Then, feeling much better, I ran like mad to catch up with Will and Robbie.

I reached them in the narrow lane that wound down to the launderette. It was a gloomy afternoon. That kind of winter afternoon gloom where all you want to do is get home. We started to run and nobody said anything. Near the bottom of the lane we passed a window where coloured Christmas-tree lights suddenly flickered on and in an instant everything looked cheery. We slowed down. "Well," Robbie said, "like, what was *that* about?"

"Search me," I said.

"Kind of impressive though," Will said, "for a girl. I mean, who would have thought Nobody Nessa could climb a tree?"

We elbowed each other as we slithered down the twisty lane. "I've been thinking, Saul," Robbie said, "you should tell the police. I mean, that's been four days now. He can't stay in the den forever."

"Robbie's right," Will said. "And now Agnes knows, and she'll tell her weirdo dad, and he'll tell the police about him, and you'll be for it."

I stopped, took a deep breath and said, "Randolph is a girl."

"What?" they said at the same time, swinging round to look at me.

I glanced over my shoulder. We had the lane to ourselves. It was now or never. "I'm not mad, ok? I know this sounds off the wall, but she almost got knocked over. She grabbed hold of me so now I'm bound to her. It's me that has to get her back. Her dad is a failure in everything. He really needs to succeed. Make the big time. So he does a bit of time travel. But, like, obviously, he's not very good at it. I mean, he got her lost. In the future, I mean. And she can't get back and I've got to help her."

"Back where?" they both asked.

"1812."

We were under a streetlight. Robbie and Will's faces were lit up ghostly orange. They looked at me like I was a raving lunatic.

"Is this for real?" Will said.

I nodded fiercely. "You saw her hair on the floor. It was me. I cut it off. I made her into a boy. I thought it would make things easier."

Will nodded. "I wondered what that was about."

"Yeah, and those are my old clothes she's got on. Her own clothes were really old fashioned."

"Funny," Will went on, "I wondered about that, too."

I was ready to hug Will when Robbie cut in. "Saul. My mum says it's hard work when you've got one baby. When you've got two at once it can drive you bananas." He gave me his pity look. "I bet you don't eat enough. I bet you don't sleep enough. I bet you don't get any peace. And I bet you don't get any attention."

"What are you saying, Robbie?" I glared at him. "You think I'm making this up? I'm not. It's true, I swear it. There's nothing wrong with me. Nothing! And we made a pact. Down by the yew tree. We swore on it, remember?"

Robbie gave a snort, shook his head and marched off. Will looked like he didn't know what to do. "Come on, Will," Robbie shouted. Will turned on his heels and scurried off.

I tore after them and grabbed at them both. "I'm not making this up. I know it's hard to believe." I was practically shouting. "Her name's Agatha Black. That's her initials in the tree and she's for real."

Robbie pushed my arm away. "If you don't tell your parents about Randolph tomorrow, I'm going to tell mine. Ok?"

"I'm the gang leader," I shouted at them both. "And I don't tell lies."

They both looked at me. "Liar," Robbie said, and they walked away.

"But this is true," I yelled and ran after them.

"Prove it," Robbie yelled back.

"Alright, I will." My heart was racing. I felt cornered. By this time we were out on the street and a few folk turned and stared at us. "But don't tell your parents," I begged. "Give me a bit more time, ok? Please. We swore on it. We're a gang."

I must have seemed really desperate. They gave me the weirdest look. I think they were a bit scared of me. "Maybe it *is* true?" Will said, glancing at Robbie. "I mean, it might be? Like, my gran saw a ghost once. Weird stuff can happen."

Robbie looked at me, all confused like he didn't know what was going on. "Ok. Three days, you sort it out, Saul, or we tell."

"Yeah," Will piped up, "cause it could be for real. I mean, I saw that red hair on the floor."

I could feel this smile of relief spreading across my face. I gave them both friendly punches on their arms then counted the dates. "December 21st, and the last day of school before the holidays," I said. "Ok, trust me on this one." And I twirled my Rasta hat in the air. "You're looking at an apprentice time traveller," I joked, catching the hat and sounding way more confident than I felt.

In the distance people were singing Christmas carols, "…Field and fountain, moor and mountain, following yonder star…" And it was starting to snow again. Then I ran off, joining in with the carol singers, singing to myself, "Oh, star of wonder, star of light…"

20

Running home through the dark white streets, I kicked up snow and whooped. I wanted Crow to show up. I was so buzzing I would have punched him on the nose, and demanded my 50p back. Then I would have told him never ever to text me again, or I would report him to the police.

When I got home, I was so fired up I could have run a marathon. Up in my room I danced around a bit then gazed out at the moon. It was nearly full. Plans whizzed round my head. I decided I would do the time travel experiment the next day. Agatha already had some of the stuff ready. I could easily get candles and matches. I had a gold star in my art jotter for a drawing I had done of the twins. I knew it wasn't real gold, but it was definitely gold coloured. And I had Macrimmon's plan. Maybe it was the full moon. Maybe it was midwinter. Or being almost the Christmas holidays. Or maybe it was because I was through with lying to Will and Robbie, but I felt like I could do anything.

And – there was something else that needed to be done. I grabbed the history prize entry form. I had almost forgotten about it. I looked at the due date. Tomorrow. I scrambled around looking for a pen and paper. I grabbed an *Oor Wullie* annual to lean on, plumped back in my beanbag seat, then twirled the pen in the air. I chewed the top of it, racking my brains trying to remember all the things Agatha had told me.

Then, I began.

This essay is by Saul Martin and it is an essay about how life really was for people in Peebles, which is a town in the Scottish borders, in the year of 1812.

I counted my words. 32. Only 468 to go. I took a deep breath, and kept writing.

A very important thing to mention is that there were no cars and there were horses and carriages but you had to be rich to have a carriage of your own so basically it meant that in 1812 people walked a lot. They ran too. They could walk and run very fast and keep going for a long time. Unless you were a vagabond because they didn't get much to eat so they sat about in the gutters spreading disease and being rude and some of them got taken off by the body snatchers who got money for bodies but if they got caught they got hanged. Hanging people for being bad is another very important thing about life in 1812. So far in this essay no cars and getting hanged are the main points.

To get hanged you get a rope around your neck and it is public so people come and watch. This will put off other robbers and murderers. Food was things like roasted chessnuts and people ate pijons and pork pies and apples and pigs were called swine. Pigs squeal when they got killed and the people killed them and even some people got to have monkeys for pets.

This is another point in my essay. Children now do not keep monkeys for pets. You might have a pet dog, or cat, or giny pig or hamster or even a goldfish in a bowl but you would never have a pet monkey in your house. But they did then.

My wrist was sore. I bet I'd never written so many words in my life. I counted them. I couldn't believe it. I had 250. I had written half the essay and I still had more to say. I felt great. I carried on.

Back in 1812 rooms in houses had different names, like parlor and drawing room and chamber. Of course they had no technology so they played cards and chess and did dancing and handwriting and men were called bucks and they joined the militia and got a red jacket. The militia is the police or army. Or they owned spinning mills. In the borders they had lots of spinning mills. Girls could not join the militia. They wore long dresses and funny hats and a very important point in my essay is girls could make fire go without matches. They had long hair. They called hair tresses. They would love to climb trees but they were to practise dancing. They were friendly people who did not travel very much. There were bullies then like we have bullies now. Life was a bit dangerous. We might think 1812 is very old fashioned but people were coming up with very modern ideas and in Peebles today some buildings still exist from 1812 and of course the river Tweed still flows now like it did then, but there is not so many fish now. The end.

I counted the words. 500! I'd done it! Then I glanced at the clock. A whole hour had passed. My stomach was rumbling. While I had been writing my essay it was like time didn't exist, which, of course, made me think about Agatha. I put the pen down, placed my essay carefully down on the carpet and stared at it. I swear it seemed to glow. "You're a winner," I murmured, smiling so hard my cheeks hurt.

Mum popped her head round the door. "Esme's teething," she said, "and Ellie's being grouchy, poor thing. Listen honey, I haven't had a minute to make dinner. I know it's dark – but you're a big boy now." She winked at me. "So could you run along to Mrs Singh and get a couple of pizzas?" She didn't notice my essay on the floor. I was going to tell her about it when she said, "Please? I'm starving. Bet you are too."

So I got ready to go out into the snow, again. I was exhausted. All that energy had gone into the essay. Now all I wanted to do was sleep. "Here's a pound for you, Saul," Mum said, pressing the coin into my hand. Then she kissed me on the cheek. "You can be a well-behaved boy when you put your mind to it." She patted me on the shoulder. "You're a good brother to Esme and Ellie. They'll be more fun when they're older. You understand, don't you, darling?"

I nodded, embarrassed. I always felt embarrassed when Mum went all emotional. Then she handed me three pounds. "Buy the cheapest," she said. "There's a two-for-one offer on margeritas."

Then I was off, trudging through the snow, keeping a lookout for Crow, and wondering what I was going to buy with my pound. I was just getting close to the shop when I heard a tune floating in the air. I looked around, but couldn't see anyone. The music was just wafting about on its own.

I walked on, feeling like I was in a dream with the dark and the snow and the music. Then I saw him – the fiddle player. He was a grungy man with a long woolly jumper and raggy beard who sometimes played old-fashioned tunes on Peebles High Street with the fiddle case open in front of him. Now here he was just near our shop, and it was like he was playing just for me. Nobody else was about. I slowed down, not wanting to pass him. The tune floated around with the snowflakes.

As he played he snapped his boots up and down on the snowy pavement. The boots had holes in them. I wanted to rush past. I took a step or two then felt him staring at me with his glinting eyes. His fiddle case didn't look very full. The last thing in the world I wanted to do was give him my pound.

I fumbled in my pocket, rubbing the warm coin. I had planned on buying juice and crisps and chewing gum. I'd given so much away I wanted to get something for myself. But the man went on playing, and all the time he fixed his eyes on me. They were the kind of eyes that could put a curse on you. Drat! I was going to feel too bad if I went by and didn't give him anything. I shuffled up and dropped the pound coin in his case. It landed with a twang, next to a 2p piece.

The man stopped playing, brought the bow to his head and nodded, like he was saluting me, then he went back to his playing. I looked down at my feet, then hurried past him, feeling the empty place in my pocket where my money used to be.

Five minutes later, when I came out of the shop with the pizzas, the man and his fiddle case had gone. Off to spend my pound, I thought, miffed, as I ran home.

That night I fell into bed. I didn't even take my clothes off. I mean, I was knackered. I couldn't believe I could do so much in one day. I sunk back onto my bed. Everything whirled in my head: the weird fiddle tune, my lost pound, Agatha and Agnes in the tree, Crow and the scary text, my new Rasta hat, my new BMX, the pizza, the essay. The essay...

I was half asleep when I got this niggling feeling that I hadn't written enough. The judges said 500 words was the minimum. And I had done the minimum. Mrs Veitch was always saying that's all I ever do – the minimum.

I never felt less like writing. I could hardly open my eyes. But the thought wouldn't go away. If I could just write two more sentences I'd have a chance. I had to do more than the minimum.

So I swung my legs onto the floor. What an effort! I slumped onto the carpet. I fished my essay out from under my bed, found a pen, scored out the words *the end* and tried to remember some more things about life in 1812.

Children did play games in 1812 like they cut out fish and banged their hand on the ground to make the fish jump so you had fish racing. The other thing they liked was making theatre shows and dressing up. They didn't have oranges unless they were rich so many children died from the meesles. They didn't have a cure for it. I hope the people in Peebles had a happy time in the past. They had their problems but basically they loved their home.

I couldn't write another word. I couldn't keep my eyes open. I couldn't even manage to write "the end".

21

Next morning, I lay in bed, remembering weird dreams. In one of them, Albert Black was getting a rope wound round and round his neck. In another dream a little monkey in a red waistcoat was crying and rubbing his eyes. I lay staring at the ceiling. It was still dark.

The first thing I heard was screeching. I thought it was the monkey. Then it dawned on me that it was Dad's taxi. That meant he had an early pick up. Next thing I heard one of the twins crying. I didn't know which one. I rolled over and something dug into my back. I still had my trousers on, and my belt. When I'd fallen asleep with all my clothes on before, I always woke in the morning with my pyjamas on. Mum had said some little pixie must have come in the night. It was her, of course, or Dad.

I fell out of bed, suddenly feeling like an idiot about the essay. Like, who did I think I was? Whoever reads it will probably have a right good laugh. I folded the paper and put it into the envelope that I had ready, but all the fizz had gone. I never won anything.

I fumbled about looking for my shoes. At least I hadn't slept with them on. My plans had seemed great last night but now in the dark morning they didn't feel so fantastic. I was ready to rip the envelope up and bin it. But some little voice inside me said: Come on, Saul, give it a try. Trying never hurts. That's what Dad always says to me. So I stuffed the essay into my rucksack.

I did a couple of star-jumps then splashed cold water on my face. Through in the kitchen I drank a huge glass of banana milk. While Mum was getting the twins up, I scooted round the living room looking for candles and matches. Usually Mum kept them hidden but now we were coming up for Christmas she had red candles on the table and a box of matches on a shelf. In the bathroom we had this little glass crystal thing. It dangled on a thread and when the sun shone it made the bathroom all rainbows. I dropped it into my rucksack.

Of course, deep down, I didn't really want Agatha Black to go. There were still loads of things I hadn't shown her, loads we hadn't done. I had told her we would go sledging. But I was starting to feel bad. She'd been in the twenty-first century for five days now. I remembered how she said the longer she stayed away, the harder it I would be to get back. But mostly it was the way she said, "I've got my life to live," that really got to me.

My rucksack was filling up. I grabbed two bagels from the cupboard and an orange. Then I scooped up a half-empty packet of chocolate biscuits and a few figs. I had learnt a few things about Agatha Black. Her sweet tooth was one of them.

I got to school just as the bell screeched. I had wanted to hand the essay in early, without anybody seeing me, but because I had spent ages getting all the time-travel equipment ready, I was going to have to do it in front of the whole class. I hung my jacket on a peg and shuffled into the classroom. Will and Robbie thumped me on the back and threw me our secret gang wink.

Mrs Veitch raced through taking the register then said, "Now, if there are any last entries for the Scottish Borders Young Historian of the Year competition, come forward and hand them in." She scanned the room. "I need to collect them now." I felt my face flush bright red. At the table at the back I saw Agnes pull an envelope out of her bag. I felt like an idiot. If she was going to enter, she would definitely win. I would probably come last. Then Dad's voice was back: trying never hurt, son...

I made a grab for my envelope and dashed forward, feeling really embarrassed. I kept looking at the ground, so I didn't see Mrs Veitch's face but Robbie told me afterwards that she practically wet herself. I hurried back to my desk and slipped onto my seat, still bright red and totally embarrassed.

"Right. Goodness! Very good. Well – er – no one else?"

I shot a glance at the back table. I saw Agnes push her envelope back into her bag.

"Well then – *bonjour, toute le monde*," sang Mrs Veitch.

"*Bonjour Madame Veitch*," we all sang back.

"And I hope you haven't forgotten: on Friday, the last day of school, it will be the shortest day of the year. Can anyone remember the name of it?"

Mrs Veitch got her second big shock of the morning. Yours-truly stuck up his hand and said, "The winter solstice!"

Agnes kept looking at me. I don't know if she was also thinking about the solstice, or if she was thinking that me and her were pals now because she'd been up a tree with Agatha. I scowled at her. At playtime she was in her usual spot by the bike shed with her usual book to hide behind. Except she wasn't reading the book. I know because it was upside down. But Will was seriously impressed by her. It was his idea that we go and hang out in the bike shed. I think he wanted to talk to her but he didn't know what to say.

While Will was staring at Agnes, Robbie was interrogating me about the essay. "I practically fell off my chair," Robbie said. "When you got up and actually handed in an *essay*! Man! I couldn't believe it. Like, no one could. Sure, Will?"

Will stopped gaping at Agnes. "Sure. Jeez, you should have seen Mrs Veitch's face. Her jaw dropped. She didn't know what to say."

"I thought she was going to have a heart attack. Serious. It was priceless. So what? You turned into some big swot?" Robbie nudged me and laughed. "I didn't even know you could read! Only joking!"

"I told you I wasn't lying." I lowered my voice because Agnes, at the other end of the bike shed, was listening. "Agatha is from 1812 and she told me all about it. I just wrote it down. It was easy. Anyway," I whispered, "I'm going to get her back there."

They gazed at me, doubtfully. "How?"

I shot a glance at Agnes who quickly looked away. I stepped in closer to Robbie and Will. "I'm going to do an experiment."

And at lunchtime that's exactly what I did.

22

When Agatha saw me burst through the gap in the hedge she clapped her hands and cheered. "Sledging time," she yelled. "I heard you coming. I was busy in my drawing. I have quite a pretty collection now. Come in and look, Saul. I have done a likeness of Agnes, yet it isna as lovely as she is."

I didn't know what to say. I'm not great at goodbyes and this was going to be one major goodbye. I smiled at her awkwardly. She must have sensed something. "Pray, what is the matter, Saul?"

I glanced down at my rucksack. Then I looked at the yew tree. I could feel this lump in my throat. We could have the picnic first, then do the experiment. "I brought bagels," I said, not looking at her but fumbling about in the bag. "They're nice. And I got you an orange. Remember, you saw one in Mrs Singh's shop – I mean, in your house, when you just arrived. Oh yeah, and I got you chocolate biscuits, and figs."

By this time Agatha was standing right in front of me. "Am I to return? Is that it, Saul? You have all in place? I am going home, is that it?"

I had the food in my hands. "We can have the picnic

first. You like chocolate. Well here, it's a biscuit. With chocolate on the top."

Agatha took the biscuit and ate it and all the time she didn't take her eyes off me. "I will miss chocolate," she said.

I knew if I was going to do this I had to get on with it. Macrimmon said you had to really want it. You had to focus your mind on the intended journey. "Your dad won't believe it when you suddenly turn up in the parlour," I said, trying to make it sound easy. "Then your monkey will screech the house down. He'll jump on your shoulders. And if that horrible Dick calls you names just tell him to get lost."

"I will," Agatha said. But she didn't look too happy.

"Remember, you've got your life to live. That's what you're always saying. But… you could stay here if you want."

"No, you are in the right, dear Saul. Of course I wish to return home. Indeed I must return home. It's only, I didna think it would be this moment. You surprise me. Have you everything ready?"

I nodded. "Finish your lunch," I said. "I'll get everything set out." Wide-eyed like she couldn't take in this was happening at last, Agatha nibbled at the bagel. I dashed into the den and brought out the plate of earth. I put it by the yew tree. I went back for the bowl of water, spilling some as I carried it. Next I hung up my glass crystal on a branch. A weak pale sun that was hardly higher than the hedge didn't do much to make bright-coloured rainbows. I pushed the glass crystal and watched it swing. So did Agatha. "It's a crystal,"

I told her, then I stuck the candle in the snow. "Hey," I nattered, waving a box of matches in the air, "this is easier than rubbing stones together. Watch!" Except it took me loads of tries before I actually managed to light the thing.

"How magical," Agatha said, but she didn't sound that impressed.

I got out my jotter, turned it to the page with the gold star, then wedged it by the tree. Agatha, sucking juice noisily from the orange, stepped closer. I could picture her frowning behind me. "It's a gold star," I muttered and looked back over my shoulder to see her gazing at my drawing.

"Pray tell, Saul, what carat gold is the star?"

"That doesn't matter, cause the main thing is," I said, getting up and practically knocking her backwards, "that you have to totally believe it's going to work." I could tell she was ready to open her mouth and argue but I rubbed my hands together. "Right then," I said, "you stand beside the tree and touch the bark." She didn't look too convinced but I patted her on the shoulder. I was sure we could trust Macrimmon's law. You had to be pure of heart, he said. Agatha Black, I could tell, was that. And you had to trust. "Believe it, ok?" I said. Agatha nodded.

"Here, Agatha, press your palms against the tree." She did. "Now close your eyes." She looked round at me, mouthed the words, "Thank you," then closed her eyes.

"The song?" she murmured. "What of the song?"

I hadn't forgotten the song. At least some good might come of giving my pound away to the busker last night. The tune he played was still going round and round in my head. "I've got one," I said. I stepped closer. My heart was pounding hard. "Are you ready?"

She nodded. She still had my clothes on, but I reckoned it wouldn't matter. I bent down and swirled the water. Next to the water the candle was flickering bravely. I stood up, closed my eyes then started to hum the tune.

I don't know how long I stood there, under the yew tree, humming that strange tune. It was like I was dreaming. I saw Mrs Singh and her red sari. I saw Agatha with her arms flung out wide. I saw the car swerve round her. And the sliding door of the cinema. And snow. And Agatha jumping hopscotch. I even saw things I'd never actually laid eyes on, like Dick pressing his nose against the window pane, and Albert Black gazing into the fire, and Pug all dressed up on market day, smoking a pipe, and Agatha scrubbing potatoes, and making paper fish flap in the air…

After what felt like ages I opened my eyes.

"It hasna worked," Agatha said. She dropped her hands from the tree, brushed passed me and walked through the snow to the den.

I ran after her. "You didn't want it enough," I shouted.

She was sitting slumped on the floor of the den, tracing a circle on the floor with her finger. She didn't look at me. "Yea havna proper gold." She sniffed and a small tear rolled down her cheek and fell onto the floor.

I left her there. I didn't know what to say. I felt like a failure. I trudged over the wasteland. I stepped in my own footsteps, going the other way. These footsteps had been confident, the ones pointing to the den. Now I felt like Albert Black, a loser. I was supposed to be an apprentice time traveller and I hadn't managed to shift her an inch.

"You look sad."

I glanced up in fright. Agnes was sitting on the wall at the edge of the wasteland. She had a hole in her shoe. She didn't seem bothered that she was sitting on the snow. I was stumped for words. She was right. I was sad. Agatha Black said I was the only one who could get her back. I had tried. I had failed. I was sad.

"I hope you win the competition." She jumped off the wall and came over to me. I was just standing there, like I had been struck dumb and frozen, all at once. "Imagine if you win, Saul. Mrs Veitch will have a hairy fit." Agnes started to giggle. "And you would get £200. Imagine that!"

The cuffs of her sweatshirt were all frayed. She could probably do with £200. She shook back her hair and smiled at me. "I'm going to see Agatha." In a funny way it felt like a relief, somebody else knowing her real name. "I won't tell anyone about the den," she said. "It's the best secret den ever. It's like a real house."

"She's done a picture of you," I said, not believing I was actually talking to this girl. She'd been in my class for years and I had never said a word to her.

"Bet she's made me look much nicer that I do." I shrugged. What was I supposed to say to that? "She's

145

pretty special, isn't she?" Agnes went on. She stared at me with her pale blue eyes. Suddenly I really wanted to tell her the truth. And the way she looked at me made it easy.

"I dunno what she told you," I mumbled. I waited for Agnes to say something but she just kept on gazing at me. "She got herself lost here. She's from Peebles, but, like, two hundred years ago. She was trying to help her dad. She's too good. She should never have agreed. Anyway, he got her lost. She nearly got knocked over by a car and that's when she found me. I was going to the shops when, wham – this girl, dressed all funny, started screaming. She grabbed me. So, she said it's up to me. I have to help her get back."

Through all this garbled speech Agnes didn't look a bit amazed or gob-smacked. She didn't look at me like I was lying, or crazy.

"So that's it," I said. "Weird, I know, but…"

"I know," Agnes said.

In the distance I heard the church bells. I had to get a move on. Was Agnes skipping school? "Um, better get back then," I muttered. Agnes just smiled again. She was the kind of girl that could be invisible. Half the time she didn't even come to school and I swear the teachers didn't notice. Will said she was so clever they couldn't teach her anything anyway.

"It's great you've been helping her." Agnes said. "Agatha told me she's having a brilliant time here. And you've fed her and showed her things."

I shrugged and went red. "We haven't done much," I mumbled. I thought about the sledging plan. We could still do it. There was a floodlight on the sledging hill. Even in the dark we could go sledging. "Um, tell her, if she wants, we could go sledging after school." Agnes looked at me, like she was waiting for an invitation but not daring to ask. "And, um, you can come too, if you like," I added, hurriedly.

"I'd love that," she said. "I haven't got a sledge, but I could watch."

Well, I didn't have a sledge either, but Will had a good one, and Robbie had two. "That's ok," I said, then I grinned and she did too. I waved to her. She waved back, then I turned and clambered over the wall. I ran all the way back to school. And even though I had tried the experiment and even though it hadn't worked, I didn't feel such a rotten failure anymore.

That afternoon I sent notes to Will and Robbie about sledging.

So can't wait

Robbie wrote on his note.

Beast

Will wrote on his.

"What's your cousin up to this afternoon, Saul?" Mrs Veitch asked.

I crumpled the notes and dropped them under my desk. I shook my head, thinking, how come she's bothered about Randolph and not Agnes? I said, "He's getting ready to go back."

"Ah, of course," she said, smiling at me. It was like I was the teacher's pet all of a sudden because I had done the essay. I squirmed in my seat and looked down. "Everyone," she said, "likes to be home for Christmas."

23

The sledging turned out to be really good fun, at least to start with. Agnes sat on the snow watching us. She didn't even have a proper coat. Then Agatha waved for her to join in and soon you'd think the five of us were the best of pals. It was really busy at the sledging hill and some of the kids from school shouted, "Hiya Randolph," to Agatha and she waved at them and shouted "Hiya" back. The same people threw us some pretty weird looks because Nessa Nobody was playing with us, but I didn't care. She wasn't nobody. She was poor, that was for sure. When we were on the sledge together I saw she had newspaper stuffed into her boots. "This is fantastic, isn't it, Saul?" she shouted as we zoomed down the hill on Robbie's sledge. It was pretty good fun. The hill was worn smooth; each time we went down it got faster and faster.

Agatha went down with Will on his big blue sledge. When we were all trudging up the hill I could hear him getting in a right state. "That was great Randolph. It was fast. Bet you don't have sledging hills in London, Agatha. I mean, Randolph. I mean, long ago."

"Much has changed, Will," she said, throwing back her head and laughing. "The river isna frozen over, but this hill is the same. The snow is the same. And we slide down it on whatever we can find. Tin trays at times."

"Cool!" Will said.

"Aye," said Agatha with a twinkle in her eye. "Cool indeed."

Robbie had all three sledges lined up for a race. Will ran down the hill. He was going to mark the finishing line and check the winner. Robbie got on one sledge. Agnes got on another and Agatha got on the third. Robbie gritted his teeth and held the rope. The girls were going to go down head first. I got the oh-so-exciting job of standing at the starting line and shouting "Ready – steady – GO!"

They zoomed down the hill, screaming and laughing. I was left at the top of the hill, cheering them on. Robbie got a good start, but then Agatha caught up fast. I watched them till I could hardly see them anymore. I pulled my Rasta hat down over my ears when suddenly I felt a snow ball land on the back of my leg. "Watcha, nerd!" I felt my blood run cold. I didn't turn round. I didn't have to. I knew who it was. The voice came closer. "Look at that. Your pals gone off and left you out in the cold, eh?"

I wished the others would come back, but I knew they'd be ages. I could still hear them laughing, way down at the bottom of the hill. I heard Crow's footsteps crunch down on the snow. He was getting closer. He was probably after more money. My heart was pounding. I wasn't going to hang about and find out what he wanted. I bolted away and ran down the hill. I fell on the glassy snow. I rolled over, and over.

Then I staggered to my feet. And I kept running.

"Agnes won," Will said and he held his hands together – inches apart, "by that much."

"What's up with you?" Robbie said, dragging his sledge over to where I was slumped down in the snow, panting like mad. I didn't know whether to tell them. "I know! You came to help pull the sledges back up? Good man! Do you want a go?" The last thing I wanted to do was go back up that hill. I got to my feet, feeling my knees throb. I shook my head. I was shivering. My gloves were damp with snow and my cheeks were numb with cold.

"Nah, it's getting late," I mumbled, "and I'm cold."

Robbie flipped open his phone and the next thing he was chatting to his mum, asking her to come and pick him up.

We all trudged along the side of the river to the car park, pulling the sledges behind us. "Here in the spring are a million primroses. Oh, it's the bonniest place then." Agatha pointed to the river bank. She had, I noticed, completely dropped the Randolph disguise.

"What's a primrose?" Will asked her.

"Oh, a dainty little pale-yellow flower. I do love the primroses." Then she started chatting away about Pug and how he would love to go sledging. Then she said she was going to tell her dad all about the modern sledges so he could make one. "That would be a safe occupation, I think," she said, laughing. "And it might bring him fame and fortune!"

The others laughed about Agatha's monkey, but not me. I kept looking back over my shoulder. I couldn't see Crow. Mind you, I couldn't see anyone. Out of the floodlight it was pitch dark. When we got to the car park, Robbie's mum was waiting with her Land Rover. It was big enough to get Robbie and his two sledges in, plus Will and his one sledge, but not big enough for all of us.

"Sorry guys," Robbie said.

"That was the best fun," Will said. Then the doors slammed and they were off. Vroooom! I suddenly felt embarrassed standing in the empty car park with two girls.

"It is dark," Agatha said, looking around her.

"And it's freezing," Agnes said, blowing into her bare hands.

After the buzz of the sledging it seemed eerily quiet. "Thanks for inviting me," Agnes said. She was looking around the car park like she was nervous about something. "I better go now."

She started to head off when suddenly this voice called out, "Agnes? Agnes? Is that you?" Next thing heavy footsteps ran towards us. Then out of the shadows the dark figure of a man appeared. "Agnes," the man said, anxiously, "I've been looking for you." I couldn't believe it. It was the grungy man who played the fiddle in the street. This was Agnes's dad.

She seemed flustered. She was looking from us to him. "I'm sorry," she said to him, "I should have told you where I was. But it's alright," and then they were gone, hurrying away and swallowed up into the dark.

"He was once a great musician," Agatha said.

"Is that what Agnes told you?"

Agatha nodded.

"It was his tune, you know?" I said.

Agatha lifted an eyebrow. "Tune?"

"That old song I was humming. You know, in the failed time-travel experiment?"

"It was a perfect song. It was not on account of the song that I failed to make the journey. I did tell you Saul. It is the gold." She marched off and I followed her. If she was heading back to the den, she was heading the wrong way.

"Where are you going?"

"Pisa."

I jerked my thumb in the opposite direction. Agatha laughed, though more of a hopeless laugh than a happy one. "So much has changed," she said, "even the very streets. Here you know, was the prison."

She was pointing to a café at the edge of the car park. I shuddered, picturing convicts grasping at bars. "Want me to walk back with you?" I said, not really wanting to. The bad thing about midwinter was that by six o'clock it was like the middle of the night.

"I would be most grateful," she said, "for alone I may wander forever."

Once we got up onto the brightly lit High Street, it didn't feel so gloomy anymore. I slowed down and tried to shake off the mood Crow had put me in. A bunch of carol singers were standing next to the Christmas tree, singing 'Good King Wenceslas', or whatever he's called. And beside the carol singers someone had a stall with hot mince pies.

I saw Agatha's nose twitch. "It reminds me of dumpling," she said, tugging at my sleeve for me to stop. "When we kept a cook she made a braw clootie dumpling. Now cook is gone I do my best. But pray Saul, why all this singing on the street? Is it market day?"

"It's for Christmas of course."

"Christmas?"

I couldn't believe she didn't know about Christmas. It wasn't what you'd call a new invention, was it? Like, the baby Jesus was born two thousand years ago. Surely Agatha Black knew that? "You know," I said, "presents and Santa, and Christmas dinner – turkey and Brussels sprouts. And decorations, and a stocking at the end of your bed. I've seen two new DVDs in Mum's cupboard, so I know I'm getting them. You must know about Christmas?"

"Turkey I know. Mr Balfour by the river keeps turkeys. I feed them sometimes. I love turkeys. I love the handsome bublyjocks and I do know of Christmas. We do sing a song for Christmas. Nothing more."

"Christmas is the best day ever," I told her. By this time the singers had moved on to 'Feed the World'. "Yeah, you can wish for whatever you want and you'll get it at Christmas." I tried to sound hopeful. Mum was dropping enough hints for me to guess I probably wasn't getting a BMX. The DVDs were probably going to be the main event.

"I wish for home. I know I complained of Dick and I know the vagabonds do steal and are foul and I know

Uncle grows weary of hapless Father. But he loves him really. He gives us his shillings. And Father loves me dearly. I miss my home, and my monkey will miss me right sore. Oh, and dear Father will be distraught with me gone." She wrung her hands together. "Oh, Saul, when all's said and done, home is home."

I pulled Agatha away from the carol singers. She was working herself up into a right state and some of them were beginning to give her funny looks. She sniffed and wiped her face with the back of her hand. Then she patted me on the arm. "I know I can trust you. All I need is gold."

"Search me," I said, patting my pockets. "I haven't got any gold. And my parents are not well off. That's what they always say. They haven't got gold kicking around."

"I need gold," she insisted, "else I will be forever lost." She turned and marched off along the High Street.

"Hey!" I ran and caught her up. "What do you want me to do? Rob a bank?"

She shook her head. "I am sorry indeed to put yea to this fuss, Saul. I amna asking you to steal gold. It would be a sin to be a robber. I will never ask yea to sin."

"Let's get a move on," I said. We hurried along the snowy street and up past the launderette, not saying any more about gold and Christmas, or anything. By the time we had reached the wasteland, a freezing fog was starting to roll in. It felt gloomy, and really cold. All the fizz and excitement of this adventure had gone.

The fog was so thick now we wandered about, looking for the hedge. We stumbled over the snow with our arms stuck out like we were playing blind man's bluff. We kept bumping into each other. This was scary movie weather and my heart was thumping. Why did I keep thinking of hangings and body snatchers? I am the gang leader, I kept reminding myself. Gang leaders are brave. I never felt less brave in my life.

I let out a yell. Something scratched my face. I jumped back. Then realised it was the prickly leaves of the holly hedge. We were close to the den. At the same time I could hear something. I felt my blood run cold. It sounded like somebody coughing.

"We have arrived at the Holland hedge that takes us through," Agatha said.

"Be quiet!" I hissed. With my heart banging I strained my ears. Had I imagined a coughing sound? I couldn't hear it now. Everything was quiet except my kicking heart. "Ok," I whispered, trying to keep my voice from trembling. I reached out my hands, fumbling to find the gap in the hedge. "Let's go."

With Agatha still clinging to my scarf we wriggled through the gap and came into the hidden wild garden. The freezing fog was so thick, by this time I could hardly see my feet. I took small steps in the direction of where I thought the den was. Agatha shuffled behind me. I took another few steps, bumped up against the den and Agatha bumped up against my back.

"Ouch! I am here," she whispered. "What…" She stopped dead and gripped my arm. The coughing noise, just inches away, sounded again. I turned rigid with fright. Somebody was in the den.

24

A white strip of light swung around inside the den. Someone was in there with a torch. My heart galloped like a bolting horse. The hacking cough came again. My face was pressed up against the side of the shed. Let it not be Crow. Let it be an old tramp. Or Will. Or Robbie.

I couldn't blink, couldn't run away. I felt frozen with fear. I couldn't see anything. All I could hear was the booming of my heart. Then I heard a voice. "Kinda creepy in here, Crow, eh? Good for me you're here." I knew that voice. It was Kyle, one of Crow's slaves. He was the one coughing. I slunk down behind the door, pulling Agatha down too. My mind raced. Now what?

Telepathy would come in handy. I pressed a finger to my lips, hoping like mad Agatha understood. She clamped her mouth shut. Frantically I pointed to the door. Agatha nodded, then folded her hands together like she was praying.

I couldn't believe this was happening. The thing I'd worried about for months had come true. Crow had discovered the den and, even worse, he was in it. Maybe he followed the footprints? He'd roped in a bit of company. I held my breath and listened.

"Kinda creepy, Crow, eh? Like, hey, really creepy." Kyle had another coughing fit.

Probably Crow had seen Agatha's dress, and the ewok. Probably he'd ripped the ears off Fred and read our graffiti names on the back of the door. My heart was thumping. What was he up to?

Kyle was still mumbling on, "Yeah, Crow, like, seriously spooksville, Crow, eh?"

Then I heard a rustle in the den. Footsteps scuffed over the dirt floor.

"Shut up Kyle." That was Crow. I saw the torch beam lurch. Someone was heading for the door. Crow probably. The beam of torch light swayed like a drunk.

I didn't move. I heard the doorknob creak. Agatha looked like she was still praying. The door opened. I slunk down, trying to disappear into the shadows. Agatha was as still as a stone.

The torch beam swung out into the fog. For a second everything was silent. I could hear Crow breathe. Then a heavy footstep crunched down right next to me. The light glared into my face. I blinked but didn't move.

"Hey, look who's here? Check that, Kyle? It's the wee gang chief. Snooping round all on his lonesome in the dark, eh? Come to visit my den. Ha!"

A scream clamoured through my brain. Aaaagh! Help!

"Hey, wee gang chief." Crow bent close. I could smell the smoke on his breath. I had my eyes closed but could see the glare of the torch through my eyelids. "You can make a choice," he growled. "Yeah, seeing as how it's nearly Christmas, me and Kyley-boy here's gonna be generous. Cause we're good like that, ain't we, Kyley-boy?"

"Yeah, too right, Crow," Kyle said, "we're really nice."

"Yeah, nice, that's right, see. Me and Kyley-boy here could heat up the place a bit." Crow laughed. "One match and this wonky place is history. Or...," he paused, "we could tie you to a tree and leave you to spend a night in ghostville. Wooo-ooo!" Kyle laughed hysterically. "Or I could be super nice and just let you go home to Mummy, then this shed's mine and if you ever come back here I'll break every window in your silly wee house. Make a choice, nerd."

I was still crouched down by the side of the shed. I felt the toe of Crow's boot nudge me in the ribs. I gasped. His choices ran round my head. They hadn't spotted Agatha beyond me. So if Crow did tie me up, Agatha could untie me. That way I'd get to keep the den. He flicked a lighter and a spark shot up. "Hope you're thinking fast, big chief. Bonfire? Night in the dark? Or I take over?" He laughed that horrible, mean laugh. "What's it to be?"

Then something happened to me. I felt this weird shift inside. It was like that blue clenched fist in my gut opened, and turned hot and red. How dare Crow come here? How dare he?

I shot a look up. With the torch on his face Crow looked evil. Kyle was tucked in behind him somewhere. Quickly I rolled my eyes to the side. Agatha had completely disappeared. I don't know how, but she'd managed to wriggle away. So I took a risk. Agatha would help me. I knew she would.

"So you two know about this place being haunted?" I was still crouched down but my voice came out steady.

"You and the ghosts together, all night long. Woooooooo!" Crow laughed again. "If you don't die of fright, you'll die of the cold, in't that right, Kyley-boy?"

But Kyley-boy just whimpered.

"I can't believe you dared to come here on your own." What was I saying? It was like all my fear had switched into courage. I wasn't even twelve yet. Crow was fourteen. But I hated feeling scared like that. All the months I'd felt scared of Crow, all the times I'd crossed over the road, or hid, just to avoid him – I was sick of it. "Yeah," I went on, lifting myself up a bit, "the ghosts here know me. They protect me. But they don't know you. They won't be too happy being disturbed. They're used to me. We have an understanding."

Crow laughed again, but there was something in his laugh that was unsure. I could hear it. Good old Agatha must have heard it too. Just at that moment there was a scratching sound behind Crow and Kyle in the den, like someone rubbing two stones together. She must have sneaked in as the boys came out.

"That's one of them," I said. "It's the ghost of the old man who lived in the big house here. It sounds like he's in the den. He looks after me, that one."

Agatha made a horrible squeaky noise. She was a better actor than I'd expected. She sounded like a pig being strangled. If I didn't know it was her, I'd be petrified, but by this time I was beginning to enjoy myself. I got to my feet.

"What do you think he's saying?" I asked.

159

Crow's face didn't look too happy. He stepped back, stood on Kyle's foot and Kyle yelped. Inside the den there was a louder squeal.

I planted my hands on my hips, like I was some cowboy in a film, "That ghost hates the kind of person who'd threaten a kid," I said pointing into the den. "Yeah, he told me he was bullied when he was young. That was two hundred years ago. But now he's dead, he's got nothing to fear, does he? If he meets a bully, he takes his revenge." Crow seemed to be shrinking before my eyes. Kyle was whimpering like a dog and clutching onto Crow's elbow, trying to pull him away. "But we can do a deal," I said. "If you leave now, I'll tell the ghost not to come after you and haunt your dreams. He's not sounding too happy." It was true: the next screech from inside the den was even more desperate. "I'd leave quick if I was you."

"Yeah," cried Kyle. "Come on, Crow, let's split."

Crow grunted and pushed Kyle away. "It's your wee side-kicks," he shouted, banging the shed door back with his foot. He spun round and flashed his torch into the den. "That's what it—"

He screamed – screamed like something was choking him. He must have seen something horrifying. He staggered back like he was going to fall, but righted himself, swung round and bolted away, with Kyle trying to clutch hold of him.

I heard them both yell as they scrambled through the gap in the hedge. I watched the torch beam jerk up and down as they fled over the snow-covered wasteland, howling into the distance. I watched until the little light was gone, swallowed up in the fog.

My knees buckled. The awful squeals had stopped. I slid down the side of the shed to the ground and started shaking. I couldn't believe what I had done. I'd got away with it. Crow would never bully me again, and he'd never come back to the den, and it wasn't set on fire, and I wasn't tied to a tree, and I wasn't mincemeat.

"Good j-job Agatha," I stammered. My teeth wouldn't stay still. "N-n-nice one!" Agatha didn't appear. "You can c-c-come out now, Agatha," I called, "they've r-r-run away."

She didn't come out. I got to my feet. My legs were like jelly. I took a step, then another one and reached the door. It was still flung right back. "Agatha?" My voice echoed eerily around the dark den. I forced myself to look into the shed but didn't have a torch, so couldn't see a thing. "Agatha?" I said it louder this time. The shed door creaked. I broke out in a cold sweat.

Agatha had gone.

25

I heard a rustling close by.

"What amusement!" I swung round. I couldn't see a thing but it was Agatha's voice. "If only girls were permitted to join a travelling theatre show."

But I still couldn't see her. "Where are you?" It was dark. It was foggy. I heard light footsteps crunch into the snow. I swung round the other way. "Good job, Agatha." It was creepy hearing her but not seeing her. "Don't freak me out. Where are you?"

The rustling sound was right next to me. It was like I was standing next to a tree. Suddenly all the dark branches fell to the ground and there she was: underneath. "Ha-ha!" she laughed. "What fun! I am a yew tree! Or, I was."

I gaped at her. She was now standing right next to me, close enough for me to see her twitching little button nose. "And I have a trick. I copied it from the travelling players. It is a frightful illusion." It was! She rolled her eyes right back in her head so all I could see were the whites. "It sent the fear of the devil into them," she said, bringing her blue eyes back, and flashing a victorious smile at me. "Ghost eyes staring out from a walking tree!"

"That's a… handy trick," I said, feeling a bit sick. It looked horrible. It was so gruesome it made twenty-first-century tricks seem babyish. "Don't do it again."

She pushed the door of the den open and went inside. "Pray they havna spoilt things," she said and set about making the fire. All I could do was flop down on a stone and watch. She was quick. It only took her about a minute and she had a little fire burning in her tin plate. Then she bustled about the den, sorting the place. She picked up Fred from the corner and brushed him down. She rushed out get her green branches, then brought them in and propped them against the wall. When she had the den cosy again she sat down on the stone opposite me and grinned. "You have majestic talent as a teller of tales," she said.

"Oh, thanks," I said. "And you're a pretty good actor, Agatha."

"Thank you." She giggled. "Ladies and gentlemen! Miss Agatha Black, the travelling player from the past!" she chanted in a dramatic voice, as if she was introducing someone famous. "And, the one and only, Master Saul Martin!" She swept her arm out towards me and bowed. "The marvellous teller of grand tales from the future!"

She laughed at that, and so did I. Suddenly, after the scariest night of my life, everything seemed really funny. It was probably the relief, but once I started laughing, I couldn't stop. I laughed so much I had tears rolling down my face. So did she. My sides ached. My shoulders shook. I didn't even know what I was laughing at anymore, but it was hilarious, and we couldn't stop, and it felt like the best thing in the world.

When I walked home that night in the dark and the fog, I wasn't one bit frightened, or one whit frightened, as Agatha would say. And later, when I flopped into bed, I imagined Agatha curled up all cosy in my sleeping bag by the fire, hearing mice close by nibbling away on crumbs of bagel. And I knew she wasn't a whit frightened either.

It was the second last day of school and Mrs Veitch said if we helped her to clear the cupboards and sort through all the felt pens and chuck out the ones that didn't work anymore, she would show us a film after lunch for a special treat.

Seeing as how I was in her good books now, I sidled up to her in the middle of the pen-sorting job and asked what kind of film it was.

"Oh, a lovely old-fashioned one," she said. "It's from a wonderful book by Charles Dickens. You remember? I've told you all about him."

I vaguely remembered but nodded like I knew perfectly. "Anyway," she went on, "you'll enjoy it, I'm sure. It's in black and white."

"Maybe I could bring my cousin," I blurted out, thinking it sounded just the kind of thing Agatha would love, and she shouldn't go back home without seeing a film. If we could ever get her home.

"Randolph all packed then, is he?"

"Yeah," I mumbled.

"Well, I'm sure we can pull up a chair for your cousin. When he goes back to London, we don't want him saying us Scots were unfriendly, do we?"

I hurtled over to the den at lunchtime. We feasted on egg sandwiches and biscuits. While Agatha ate, I told her about the film.

She didn't look too pleased.

"It's old fashioned," I said, "like a play, and it won't be violent or noisy. And it won't smell." Of course, I didn't actually know what it would be like. "It'll be great fun," I said, polishing off the last biscuit.

"Will Agnes be there?"

"I suppose so," I said, trying to remember if she had been at school that morning.

"Her father looked greatly perturbed."

"What's that supposed to mean, Miss Big Words?"

Agatha laughed. "Unhappy. All jumpy. Fretful. Anx–"

"I get it," I said. "So, you coming?"

She bit her nail for a moment but in the end I convinced her to at least give the film a try. "You can just close your eyes if it frightens you," I said.

As we ran over the wasteland I tried to explain how films work. Agatha looked baffled. "Sledges I understand," she said.

"Yeah, well, it takes a bit of getting used to," I explained, hoping like mad she wasn't going to scream or faint or burst into tears.

"We've reserved the best seat in the house for you, Randolph," said Mrs Veitch. "Come on up here now. Don't be shy." She beckoned for Agatha to sit right at the front.

"He can sit beside me," I called out. "He doesn't…"

"Nonsense." Mrs Veitch sat poor Agatha down and told everyone else to be quiet. I was at the back, watching Agatha glance around, looking for Agnes probably.

The room went dark. A whirring noise started up. It got louder. Numbers flickered on a screen. Violin music blared. A trumpet sounded. The words

A Christmas Carol

flashed up onto the screen. Some children cheered. Mrs Veitch told them to settle down.

I was biting my bottom lip so hard I could taste blood. I kept my eyes glued to the back of Agatha's head. I saw her hands clamp over her ears. I heard her gasp. I could pretty much bet her eyes were shut tight. She sat so rigid I doubt she was even breathing.

For an hour and a half she stayed that way. Mrs Veitch was so glued to the film, I don't think she noticed. After about ten minutes of me holding my breath and not seeing anything of the film, I started to relax. Agatha wasn't going to scream. She wasn't going to fall off her chair. I unclenched my fists, and watched the screen between bursts of checking on Agatha.

I'm a modern boy. I liked the film, even though it was a bit old-fashioned.

In the commotion afterwards, when Mrs Veitch put on the lights and wound up the screen, I grabbed Agatha by the wrist and whisked her out.

"Sorry about that," I said when we were safely out in the playground.

"Oh, but it was a marvel indeed," she said. "I did hear the speaking voices. Sometimes I peeped between my fingers and saw the moving pictures. Oh, I am right glad that Mr Scrooge came good in the end. I wept for the lame little Cratchet. Didna you?"

"But, I thought you were totally freaked out by it?"

"I am adapting to the future," she said, and winked at me. "But pray, tell me, now that Mr Scrooge has given charity to Mr Cratchet, the lame little boy will grow stronger, won't he? Please, say he will? Oh! I couldna bear it if he weakens and dies. I fear my heart will break."

"He'll be ok," I assured her.

She looked seriously relieved. "Thank heavens."

Just then Will and Robbie came charging across the playground. "You had your hands over your ears half the time," Robbie yelled, giving Agatha a high-five. Then he swung round and gave me a high-five. "We heard," he said, and whistled. "Word's out you stood up to Crow."

"Yeah," said Will. "You're the best Saul."

I shrugged and looked at Agatha. "Well, I got some help." Then Will and Robbie turned their admiring looks onto Agatha.

"I just rolled my eyes," she said. "Saul was the one who put the fear of God into him." Then she looked around. "Pray, where is Agnes? Do you know?"

Robbie shook his head.

"She sometimes has to stay at home and look after her granny," said Will.

Robbie and me stared at him. "How come you know so much?" we asked.

"My granny told me."

"And where is Agnes's home?" Agatha asked him.

"Dunno," Will mumbled, except he looked like he did. "I think maybe they stay in a caravan – er – behind the petrol station."

Me and Robbie threw each other a look. Everybody in Peebles knew about the caravans behind the petrol station. Even Crow would give them a wide berth. Fancy Agnes living there!

"Let us go then." Agatha looked eagerly at me, then Robbie, then Will.

The three of us shrugged. We looked at our feet. We scratched our heads. We coughed.

"Ok," said Will. "Let's go!"

26

It was half past three in the afternoon, and already it was starting to get dark. Of course, it was going to the caravan site that was freaking me out, but the dark didn't exactly help. "It's a long way," I said, dragging my heels. "It'll take ages. And it's going to be dark soon. Like, really dark."

But Agatha was striding ahead next to Will, along the gritted pavement that headed out of Peebles. Robbie and I looked at each other, frowned, and followed them. "I think she's really old," Will was telling Agatha. "My gran says she's about ninety-five."

Agatha was nodding her head. Boy could she walk fast when she wanted to. I was practically having to run to keep up. "As I am going home soon," Agatha announced, to all of us, "it wouldna feel proper to leave without bidding her farewell. I have also happily made your acquaintance," she smiled at the three of us, "but Agnes is the only girl I have made a friend of in the future."

We were hurrying past the sign that said

**Welcome to Peebles,
historic Borders town,
winner of Scotland in Bloom 2005**

The garage was in sight. Its bright neon sign blazed in the dim December afternoon. Agatha, I noticed, wasn't doing as much gazing around as usual. Maybe she was getting used to bungalows and streetlights and cars and buses, or maybe she was in a terrible hurry?

"Slow down," I said, panting. It wasn't that I was knackered, but we were practically at the creepy caravan site. Robbie wasn't looking too happy either. I could see him fiddling with his phone, like he was about to tell his mum to come and pick him up.

"Right, well, we're here," Will said, and he wasn't sounding too ecstatic either. "Um, I think there's a way in over there." He pointed to the car wash.

Me and Robbie stared at him. "Behind it," Will explained and led the way.

Agatha hurried by his side and me and Robbie followed, our shoulders bumping up against each other. "If things get nasty," Robbie whispered, "I'll phone the police."

Agatha looked back, waving for us to hurry up. Keeping close together we slipped round behind the car wash and suddenly there it was. The place looked like a tip. One streetlight shone down on three caravans, two old vans and a broken-down rusty sports car. It wasn't what you'd call a holiday caravan site. It was more like a dump. The snow was slushy, but I could see someone had made a snowman. It had a brown woolly hat on. I recognised that hat. I was pretty sure the fiddle player had worn it.

A light glowed at the window of one caravan. The other two caravans were in darkness. "Why do they live here?" Robbie hissed in my ear. He sounded seriously worried. "Like, why would anybody want to live here?"

Will shrugged. I was going to say something about homeless people, when suddenly music floated out into the air. "It's him and his fiddle," Will whispered. "Listen!"

We did. Agatha, Will, me and Robbie just stood still and listened. We looked like statues, or people under a spell. The fiddle music floated around and around us. "It is wondrous," Agatha said, "Mother used to love that tune."

"Agnes!" Her dad stopped playing the music. Now I could make him out. He was a dark shadow sitting on the caravan step. "Agnes, come out here." He didn't sound as worried as he had the day before. "I think it's your friends from school."

I heard some voices inside the caravan. Agnes appeared on the caravan step. Because everything was pretty dark I couldn't make out faces clearly, but I guessed Agnes was probably looking pretty embarrassed. "Dear Agnes," Agatha called out, "Oh, dearest Agnes," and dashed towards her. Agnes' dad shuffled out the way and disappeared back into the caravan. I watched as Agatha hugged her like a long lost sister. "I couldna let myself go without bidding yea farewell."

Me, Will and Robbie just stood outside, not knowing what to do or where to go.

"Agnes?" A woman called from inside the caravan. This must be her granny, I thought. "Bring them in," the old woman shouted. "I'll put on the kettle, and maybe we've a biscuit kicking about somewhere. Don't just stand there, lassie, invite them in!"

That is how me and Will and Robbie got ourselves invited into Agnes's caravan. By the time we all filed in, there were seven of us. "Well, isn't this a party," the old woman said. She was fishing about in a cupboard looking for cups. She didn't look ninety-five.

"Take a seat, if you can find one," Agnes's dad said. Agnes looked delighted and ashamed, all at the same time. Sometimes she couldn't stop smiling and sometimes she jumped up and brushed crumbs away or plumped up a cushion. Her dad just sat in the corner putting waxy stuff on his fiddle bow. There was something cosy about the caravan, even though it was a bit dirty and a bit messy and a bit crowded. Robbie wouldn't lean back on the chair and I knew he was still fiddling with his phone inside his pocket. But Will was pretty cool. Agnes's dad started playing the fiddle again and Agnes sang along with him. Will played a drum that the old woman gave him and Agatha just looked delighted. It was like a little party.

The old woman found a packet of shortbread and passed them around. I saw Robbie examining his. "Just eat it," I whispered, when everyone else was singing. "It's not going to kill you." And he did, and he started to loosen up, and next thing me and him were shaking a jar of lentils each.

"That's a poor man's percussion," Agnes's dad said, and laughed.

And for about an hour, in the cosy wee caravan, we had a ceilidh. That's what Agnes's gran called it. She hummed along and drank about three cups of tea. Over the rim of her tea-cup she was often staring at Agatha.

It was Robbie – typical – who broke up the party. "I have to go," he said, standing up and looking at me and Will like we should go too.

"A song from Agatha first," Agnes said, waving for Robbie to sit down again.

"Mother's favourite song then," said Agatha. She stood up, closed her eyes and sang. Agnes's dad, who I'd learnt by this point was called Michael, played along with her. It was an old Scottish ballad about a swan flying over a frozen loch, and half the words I didn't understand but the way Agatha sang it was beautiful.

"Lovely! Oh, just lovely." Agnes's gran thought so too. A tear trickled down her face. "It was my own mother's favourite song," she said, once Agatha finished, "and I havna heard it in years." The old woman looked at Agatha then reached over and took her hand. "Thank you," she said, nodding her head, "thank you."

I got that strange prickle up my spine again. I looked at Agatha. I looked at Agnes. I looked at the old woman. And I understood something that Agatha had probably known all along.

"You ok?" Robbie nudged me.

"Yeah." I shook my head. I thought if I stood up I might fall down. I could see Agnes was shaking out a blanket. The candles had burned down. The old woman was yawning, though it was only about six o'clock. Michael was draining the dregs from his tea-cup. Will was putting his cup into a basin.

"Agatha can sleep here tonight," Agnes said. "I've made rabbit stew. She can have some."

"That will indeed be scrummy," Agatha said, already unlacing her boots.

I wanted to say, What about the den? But it sounded silly. What did I think? That Agatha Black would live forever in our den? So I just smiled at her. "Night then, Agatha," I said.

"Good night to you, Saul," she said. "Sleep soundly."

27

After we'd said goodnight to everybody, me, Will and Robbie left the caravan site and went back round by the car wash and through the garage. Like I said, it was only about six o'clock but it felt much later.

"She isn't ninety-five," Robbie said when we were back on the road. "Not even anywhere near it."

"Yeah, and she doesn't look ill," I added.

"It wasn't as bad in there as what you would expect, eh?" Robbie said.

"Actually," Will said, "I wouldn't mind living in a caravan like that." We stomped on, kicking up snow and bumping into each other.

"It's not as good as Pisa though." Robbie stopped and looked at us both. "Is it?"

Me and Will agreed, even though the caravan was cosy, it wasn't as good as Pisa.

We stomped on a bit more and soon reached the street corner. This was where we went off in different directions. But nobody was rushing away. We lingered by the low stone wall of a house that had a sign in the garden telling Santa to stop here.

"Only five days till Christmas." Robbie punched the air. "Can't wait."

"Totally." Will smacked his hands together to keep warm.

"Which means," Robbie said, elbowing me in the ribs, "it's just one day till 21st December. Remember Saul? You can't go leaving Agatha in our den forever, or in that caravan. You said you'd get her back." Now he patted me on the shoulder. "You scared Crow off. That's ace."

"Yeah, totally ace," added Will.

"So," Robbie went on, "getting Agatha home should be a cinch."

My gang was looking at me like I was some kind of hero. Crow had given me a wide berth earlier that day, like he was scared of me. I really had scared him off. It *was* ace. They were right. "I'm working on it," I said, grinning. "Meanwhile, any idea where I could get some gold?" They frowned. "Pure gold," I added. "It's got to be pure."

"Oh, hang on." Robbie started patting his pockets. "Think I've got a few bars stacked away somewhere."

Will giggled. "Or we could break into Edinburgh Castle and nick the Crown Jewels."

"Yeah, good plan," I said. "Any other brilliant ideas?"

They were trying to work out if I was joking or not. I could tell by the way Robbie chewed the inside of his cheek and Will scratched his nose. I lowered my voice. "It's for protection. Agatha's dad didn't give her enough gold. That's why she got lost. I've got everything else to get her back home, but I need gold."

"The dentist!" Will beamed. "She could get her tooth filled while she's here, and the dentist can give her a gold filling."

"Na," Robbie said dismissively, "dentists charge a fortune for gold fillings."

We took his word for it. I had been secretly hoping Robbie would come up with the gold, but even he, it seemed, wasn't that rich. "Sorry mate," he said. "I mean, if I find some kicking about, I'll sling it your way, ok, Saul?" He winked at me and laughed.

Just then a woman appeared with bags of shopping then turned into the garden of the house we were standing in front of. She was puffing and panting and we all fell silent and watched her. She put her heavy bags down on the garden path, shook her wrists then waved at us. "And what's Santa bringing you boys for Christmas, then?"

"A skateboard, a laptop and an iPhone," said Robbie, reeling off just three things from his list.

"Clothes and stuff," said Will, "and maybe a camera."

"Stuff," I mumbled and waited for her to go in the house. She took a while but soon as I heard the door click, I said, "I think they could be related."

"Yeah," Will said, "I worked that out too."

"Who?" Robbie said. "That woman and Santa?"

Me and Will giggled and both shook our heads. "No. Agatha and Agnes, that's who."

"And the granny as well," Will said. "Maybe even the dad."

Robbie whistled. "Well, Agatha better get back then, because if she doesn't make it back…"

"They won't exist," Will and me said at the same time.

We were all silent then. A few snowflakes swirled around like tiny ghosts in the streetlight. The Santa stop here sign was dusted white. Agnes, I thought, was the kind of person who might just disappear and people would say, "Agnes? Who was she?" I shivered.

"I was wondering," Will said, stamping his feet on the snow, "if Agnes could join our gang?"

"Thought we said three…" Robbie began.

"Yeah," I cut in, "that was then. Things change."

"My gran says that's just what she needs."

"What?" Robbie said, "a gang?"

Will shook his head. "Friends."

They both looked at me while I frowned like I was considering it. "Ok," I said eventually, "I say she can." And just at that moment the woman in the house must have flicked on her Christmas lights because suddenly the whole place lit up.

28

The next day was the last day of school! Yeeesssss!

It was also the winter solstice. I knew because Mrs Veitch had gone on about it so much. When I woke up I heard the snow shift on the roof. My first thought was that if the snow melted, Agatha's snow angel would vanish. My second thought was the history essay – today was the prize ceremony.

But I didn't have much time to get myself worked up about that because next thing Mum burst into my room, bounced Ellie down on my bed and sighed. "Look after your sister, will you. Make sure she doesn't roll off the bed. Esme's been sick all over her cot, and your dad is out and I didn't sleep a wink. They were crying all night."

She hurried out, sighing some more. Ellie wasn't crying now. She was gurgling and chuckling and punching at my head. I bounced her up and down on the bed and she chuckled and made ga-ga noises. "Any idea where I might get my hands on some gold?" I said, rubbing my nose against her tiny smooth nose. She punched me again. I got out of bed, picked her up and showed her the snowman out the window, in the dark pink dawn light. Except the snowman had definitely got smaller. "It's turning into a snow baby," I said. She stopped chuckling and gazed out. We stayed like that, me and my wee sister, silent, watching the snow baby in the garden.

"Ahhhh." She smiled and reached towards the window pane.

"I know," I said, "Ahhhh. Snow's beautiful, Ellie."

When Mum came into my room ten minutes later to get her, she didn't mention the history competition. Probably she forgot. Or maybe she'd thought I'd just been joking about doing it. Parents were allowed to come to the Christmas assembly, but I didn't invite them.

Later, as I slithered along the street on my way to school I smiled to myself, which helped with the butterflies in my chest. "Ahhhh!" I shouted, thinking of Ellie and crunching my feet down into the white packed snow. I took a deep breath. "Right! Last day of school – Ahhhh!"

Once inside I wasn't so cheerful. I hung about near the back of the school hall. There were a lot of Christmas carols to get through, and the minister came in and spoke about there being no room in the inn. I kept glancing about, looking for Agatha and Agnes but there was no sign of them.

"They're probably up a tree," Robbie whispered, nudging me.

Mrs Veitch gave a little talk about the three wise men and how Christmas is a time of giving. I only started to listen when she said one of the three wise men from the east brought the baby Jesus gold. Robbie heard that too and dug me in the ribs. "You, me and Will," he whispered. "We're the three wise men. Pisa's the stable."

I tried not to laugh. Especially because just then the head teacher, Mr Wilson with the bushy eyebrows, stood up and scanned the packed hall. My heart thumped. "And now... it is... time," he said, incredibly slowly, "... to turn our thoughts to this year's Scottish Borders Young Historian of the Year award." I looked down at a chewing gum stain on the floor. "I am pleased to say eight pupils from Kingsland entered this year and, I may add, did rather well, too." Robbie nudged me again. I glanced over my shoulder. The high school had finished up the day before and a few big brothers and sisters had come in and were hanging about at the back of the hall. A few parents had also come in. I recognised Agnes's grandmother. She waved at me. Maybe she thought Agnes had gone in for the competition.

I couldn't see any sign of Agnes though, or Agatha. Up at the front, Mr Wilson was droning on about old buildings in Peebles and the Beltane celebrations and the ancient customs still alive today, such as crowning the Beltane queen. I felt my hopes sink. I hadn't written anything about that. Then he spoke about the noble stories of Sir Walter Scott and then about the ancient history of Neidpath Castle. I'd forgotten all that too.

"Saul!"

I glanced over my shoulder. Agatha was standing at the back waving at me. She was next to Agnes and

Agnes's grandmother. Agnes waved too. I nodded at them. Then I heard the door of the assembly hall open and my dad slipped in to stand at the back. He caught my eye and winked. My heart thumped again, hard.

"Your fan club's arrived," Robbie whispered in my ear.

Mr Wilson had finally stopped going on about old castles. "Of course, many schools in the Borders took part. I would like to congratulate everyone who made the effort. Well done." He smiled down on us all. Then he clapped, followed by a ripple of applause. Then he coughed and the applause died away. "Now, I would particularly like to mention the three placed entrants that come from this school. So, without further ado, in tenth place, describing the wonderful history of the mills along the river: Darcy Jenkins, Primary 6." There was a great round of applause as Darcy was ushered to the platform to receive a prize. It looked like a book.

"In fourth place, describing the history of sport in the Borders, especially rugby, we have, from Primary 5, Eirinn Grant." Another huge round of applause as a boy, led by his beaming parents, collected his prize. Another book.

"And now, I am very pleased indeed to announce some exciting and gratifying news. The choice, I am told by the judges, was indeed a hard one, because they received so many fascinating essays. But they have awarded first prize to an entry from our very own Kingsland Primary School!"

Robbie poked me in the ribs. I shuffled away from him and stared at the floor. My heart was thumping like mad. I didn't want to hope, but I couldn't help hoping. Will was punching me on the arm and smiling.

"One of our students wrote of life in this very town in times gone by. The essay was written with such freshness that, I quote the judges… 'We who read it felt ourselves transported back to a time before cars roared through our streets, before electric lights glared day and night, before supermarkets and computer games and even schools and hospitals were taken for granted.' Ladies and gentlemen, girls and boys, the first prize of £200 goes to a Primary 7 student…"

Robbie nudged me.

So did Will.

I stared at my shoes.

"Saul Martin!"

"It's you!" Robbie gasped. "Oh my God, it's you. I can't believe it! Go and get it!" I didn't move. Robbie clapped me on the back then he pushed me forward. So did Will. Other people starting clapping and cheering.

It was Dad who steered me up to the platform. My legs felt wobbly. I don't know how I managed to walk. Mr Wilson was stretching his big hand towards me and in a total daze I clambered up onto the platform and shook it. Then he handed me the envelope with two hundred pounds cash in it. "Thank you," I mumbled. I said it again, "thank you." My hands trembled. I couldn't believe it. I had won!

Mr Wilson wouldn't let me jump down off the platform. He handed me a sheet of paper. He patted me on the shoulder. Would I, he said, do them the great honour of reading out my prize-winning essay?

I gazed down. Robbie and Will and Agatha and Agnes had all come to the front. Dad stood next to them giving me the thumbs up. The paper shook in my hands. Everyone was gazing up at me like I was a superstar. I coughed.

"Go on, darling." That was Mum. Where had she come from?

I stuffed the prize money in my pocket. I took a deep breath. I hoped my voice wasn't going to wobble. I said…

This essay is by Saul Martin and it is an essay about how life really was for people in Peebles, which is a town in the Scottish borders in the year of 1812.

I paused and looked over the top of the paper. Agatha was gazing up at me. I saw a small tear run down her face. I kept going.

A very important thing to mention is that there were no cars and there were horses and carriages but you had to be rich to have a carriage of your own so basically it meant that in 1812 people walked a lot. They ran too. They could walk and run very fast and keep going for a long time.

I kept reading. I wasn't nervous anymore. At the end of each sentence I glanced at Agatha. She was gazing up at me, her blue eyes like huge pools. Agnes stood by her side.

They didn't have oranges unless they were rich, so many children died from the meesles. They didn't have a cure for it.

Then I paused and looked at Agatha. I was nearly at the end of the essay. Because I knew the last bit by heart I looked over the top of the paper and spoke the words straight to her.

I hope the people in Peebles had a happy time in the past. They had problems like we do too but basically they loved their home.

"The end," I added, and I couldn't stop myself smiling. I had done it, and I could feel that fat envelope heavy in my pocket.

"Bravo!" shouted Agatha and everybody started clapping and cheering again. Agatha was smiling with a tear in her eye. In that moment I knew exactly what I was going to do with the money.

29

The prize ceremony was over and I stepped down from the platform.

"Son! That was fabulous," Dad hugged me, crushing the fat envelope between us. "Brilliant. I loved the bit about the flapping fish and the squealing pigs." Then Mum hugged me. "Christmas came after all!" she said. "Well done, Saul, I'm so proud of you."

Then Agnes came dashing up to me. Only now I noticed she looked totally different. It looked like Agatha had given her a haircut. "That was fantastic," she said.

"Yours was probably loads better," I said.

Agnes shook her head. "Not a bit. Yours was real."

Up at the front of the hall the choir had started singing – "We wish you a merry Christmas" – and a few red balloons floated up to the ceiling. I could smell hot mince pies. School was out and everyone was cheering. In all this buzz, Agnes stood quietly in front of me, with Agatha by her side.

"Hey, Agnes?" I said, "want to join our gang?"

Her jaw fell open and her pale blue eyes widened. "She certainly does," Agatha said putting an arm around her shoulder. Agnes looked so stunned she could only nod her head.

Next thing my gang appeared, right next to me. Robbie and Will slapped me a high-five, then Agnes. "Hey," I said, turning to Robbie and Will, "why don't you two go with Agatha and Agnes to the den? They can show you how to make fire without matches."

"Sure thing," they immediately replied.

"I'll be there in half an hour," I said. "There's something I need to do first."

"Sure," they chorused again as I turned and threaded my way out of the packed hall. Before I reached the door, about a hundred people had shouted, "Well done, Saul!"

I waved to Mum and Dad and ran out of the school and through the streets, the fat envelope with a whole £200 clenched in my hand. The sun had come out. The sky was blue and the white world sparkled.

I dashed over the road, up the Northgate, looking for number 79. My heart was thudding. I ran all the way to the quiet end of the street. Then I saw it: a tiny shop with three gold balls over the door.

I slowed down. I was panting hard. Looking in the window I felt this thud of disappointment. I thought a gold shop would be special but this place looked like a junk shop. There were loads of china teapots and necklaces and milk jugs and stuff. But then, beside a guitar, I saw it, lying on a tiny scrap of purple velvet – a small gold ring. Next to it there was a piece of paper with the words *Pure gold* written on it. This was it! This had to be the gold that would help Agatha get home.

I burst into the shop. A bell tinkled and the man seated behind the counter looked up. He had a white pointy beard and white hair down to his shoulders. "Ah! Good morning young man," he said, "and what can I do for you?"

"The gold ring," I blurted out, pointing to the window, "I want it."

"Ah," said the man again, lifting his glasses up to peer at me, "that one?" Then he shook his head. "I have other pretty rings." He came out from behind the counter. With his little round glasses and pointy beard it was like he had stepped out of a wizard film.

"How much is it?" I asked. "The pure gold one? The one on the purple velvet?"

"Too much," he replied, shaking his white head. "You might be interested in these?" He whisked a couple of rings out of a glass cabinet but I shook my head.

"No. It's that one I want." I pointed again. "It says it's pure gold, and it looks like the perfect size." I lifted my envelope up. "I've got money. I just won the history prize. I wrote an essay about Peebles in 1812."

The man's face creased into a smile. "Isn't that marvellous?" He went over to the window, fumbled about, pushed aside the guitar and eventually brought out the pure gold ring. He breathed hard on it and rubbed it on his sleeve. "Pawn shops are sad places," he said, more to the ring than to me. "People sell their dreams." Then to my amazement he put the ring back in the window. "Save your prize money. I'm hoping the old woman raises enough money to buy her granddaughter's ring back. It's a bonny one. Old too, very old."

"But I need it. How... how much is it?" I stammered.

He stared at me, made little clucking sounds, then said, "I'd let it go for £180, I suppose."

"I'll take it," I said, tearing open my envelope.

The man looked unsure, but he nodded then wrapped the ring in the purple scrap of velvet. "Dreams for sale," he said, handing it towards me. At the same time he opened his other hand, waiting for the money. I put £180 into his hand and quickly he wrapped his fingers over the notes. Then he let me have the ring.

He stuffed the money into his till, muttering how a pawn shop was the saddest place on earth. "History, eh?" he said, as I made for the door, clutching the precious ring in both my hands. "There's a lot of history and broken dreams here." He swept his arm round the shop – at the guitars, clarinets, golf clubs, necklaces, bracelets, china plates and rings.

I opened the door. The bell tinkled. "Merry Christmas," I shouted then dashed out into the street and headed for the sweet shop.

30

I was sure I'd been away longer than half an hour. I hurried over the snow-covered wasteland but kept stopping every two minutes to check the purple velvet was still in my pocket, and the gold ring was still in the velvet. As I got closer to the den I sniffed wood smoke in the wind. The wind on my cheek, I noticed, wasn't biting cold like it had been.

By the time I reached the secret gap in the hedge I could hear Robbie, Will, Agatha and Agnes laughing in the garden. I wriggled into the gap but didn't step through. Feeling like a spy, I looked and listened. The fire was burning bright. The four of them were standing with their backs to me and Robbie was flinging twigs into the fire. "Our gang is the best," Will was saying, "and we do ace games."

"Yeah," Robbie piped up, "it's totally amazing. We're always having adventures and playing pirates and robbers and spies and soldiers. It's the best fun."

Good old Robbie. I smiled at that, glad I had bought his favourite sweets. Meanwhile my time-traveller's mind was racing. We had the fire blazing. We had earth and air. I had a bottle of water. The crystal still hung from the tree, and now that the sun was shining we'd get rainbows galore. The fire smoke made vapours. We had the yew tree. I remembered Michael's song. And for the umpteenth time I patted my pocket. I had the gold!

Agnes was laughing. "I'm going to love this gang so much," she said. "Oh, and we could trap rabbits and skin them and roast them and have picnics and midnight feasts."

I heard Robbie make a loud, "Yuk," noise. Agatha laughed.

I saw Will turn to Agatha and say, "You were already kind of in the gang as Randolph. So, I mean, if you're hanging around, you can join again as Agatha."

I stepped out and strode down the garden. "Agatha's going home," I announced, and they all swung round to look at me.

"Really?" said Agatha, wide-eyed. She dropped the twig that she'd had in her hand.

"Really," I said, hoping this time it was. Then I tossed packets of jelly babies and midget gems to Robbie. I handed Agatha a tangerine. I gave Agnes a box of Maltesers and I gave Will a huge bag of smoky bacon crisps.

"Hey!" shouted Robbie, "The rich brainy kid is here to feed the poor," and he crammed half the packet of jelly babies into his mouth.

We all sat down on the log to tuck into our feast. I bit into a Milky Way and watched Agatha unpeel the tangerine then eat it, segment by segment, as if it was the most delicious thing she'd ever tasted. "Yummy, scrummy," she said, licking her lips.

Will munched on a few crisps, looking very thoughtful. "Is Agatha really going home?" he asked.

"Back to 1812," I said, drawing the purple box from my pocket.

"Back to the body snatchers and the monkeys?" asked Robbie, his mouth full of jelly babies, "And the market days and the pigeon pie?"

"And the flapping fish?" asked Will, "And the games of cards and pipe smoke?"

"That's right," I said, feeling a lump in my throat after I'd already swallowed the Milky Way.

"Yes," said Agnes, "all of that, and then there'll be the growing up." She took Agatha by the hand and looked at her. "When there'll be the dancing with the bonny gallants and you'll marry one of them, the very best one, and have children."

"And grandchildren," said Agatha who looked like she didn't know whether to laugh or cry. She licked the last bit of tangerine from her lips. Her face was flushed. Her eyes shone. "And great-grandchildren, and great-great-grandchildren." She smiled at Agnes and whispered, "and great-great-great-great-grandchildren."

Agatha tugged Agnes up onto her feet and the two of them spun round and round in the snow. Flakes whirled up, then they fell back, laughing. "Let's make an angel," Agatha shouted and flipped her arms up and down. Agnes did the same. Robbie and Will threw a few snowballs at each other and ate more sweets.

Meanwhile I got busy. I placed the bottle of water by the yew tree. For a moment I stared at the letters carved there: AB It struck me how it was the beginning of the alphabet – like the beginning of everything. I pushed the crystal and watched it sparkle and swing.

It didn't take long to set everything else up. I took a deep breath then called to Agatha, "If you really want to go home, it's time now."

"One moment," she called, grabbing Agnes by the arm and pulling her into the den. In minutes, they'd stepped back out. Agnes was dressed in my blue trousers and red hoodie. She was carrying the old coat Mrs Singh had given Agatha that day she arrived. "The coat is for my dad," she said.

Agatha was wearing the clothes I had first seen her in, except of course, the long red hair was gone. "Now I am ready to go home," she cried and stepped towards me. Her pocket, I saw, was crammed full of drawings. I spied the top of the Christmas card I had made for her.

"Wow!" Robbie and Will cried. "You really are old fashioned. This is seriously for real."

"What did I tell you?" I said, my mind leaping about for how to involve them.

"What do you want us to do?" asked Will.

I thought of Macrimmon. "If you could stand just outside the hedge and make sure no one comes in, that would help us focus. And imagine like mad that this is going to work, ok? Picture Agatha back home, two hundred years ago."

They nodded eagerly, like they were glad to have a job to do and, ran towards the hedge waving to Agatha.

"Bye, Agatha," they both shouted, "it was great to meet you. Have a merry Christmas in 1812!"

"It was great to meet you too, dear Robbie, dear Will,"

she called. "I will have a right merry time, be sure of that."

Robbie and Will hurried off to stand like bouncers by the entry to the garden.

Then me and Agatha and Agnes made our way over to the yew tree. Agnes, with her haircut, now looked spookily like Agatha. We walked over the snow, which was beginning to turn slushy, in silence. I saw Agatha gazing at her initials in the trunk.

I took the ring out of the box. It felt warm. "Right," I said. It was like my heart was in my mouth. "We'll do what we did before, except this time it's going to work." I slipped the ring onto Agatha's middle finger. It fitted perfectly.

She gasped. "Oh Saul, oh mercy. Bless you!"

Agnes stared down at the ring, and smiled. "Goodbye, dear Agatha," she said, "and thank you so much. Thank you for visiting, thank you for everything."

"Thank you," said Agatha. "It isna every day you meet your great-great-great-great-great-grandchild, is it?" Then she turned to me and smiled her widest smile. "And it isna every day I meet a courageous and wondrous boy such as you. I will never forget you, dear Saul. Never ever. Goodbye."

"Goodbye Agatha," I said, swallowing hard. She smiled at me and I hardly knew what I was doing, but I gave her a big hug, then let her go.

Agatha stretched her arms out to the side. The sun caught the gold ring, flashing dazzling bright rainbows all over the garden. She turned in a slow circle, as though she was taking notes for the very last time. The den. The white hills of the Borders. The empty land where her grandfather's house had once stood. The fire in the middle of the garden. Her snow angel. Agnes's snow angel. The hedge where Robbie and Will were. And Agnes and me.

She looked like an angel herself. I felt tears in my eyes. This was it. I knew after today I'd never see her again. Slowly she brought her arms down by her side, looked at me and nodded.

"Ready?" I said. We stepped towards the yew tree. She stretched out the hand with the ring on it and placed it against the bark of the tree. I put my hand over hers and Agnes put her hand over mine. "Believe it," I whispered.

In front of me, Agatha stood tall. "I do," she whispered, "with all my heart, I do," and with a shiver up my spine, I started to hum the old tune.

I felt the warmth of Agatha's hand under my palm. I felt the wind on my cheeks. I could smell the wood smoke. I heard a robin chirp. The crystal flashed. I heard the water in the bowl stir and splash of its own accord. Still I hummed the tune and it was as if the tree itself shuddered. Goosebumps ran up and down my spine. I felt my eyelids droop.

I don't know how long I was there, singing and wishing and believing. Slowly I became aware of a drip-drip-drip sound. I stopped humming. What was it going drip-drip-drip? Tears? Or snow melting from the branches?

In the distance I heard the church bell strike one o'clock. I could feel the sun warm the back of my neck. I felt the rough bark of the yew tree under the palm of my hand. I felt the warmth of Agnes's hand resting on the back of my hand. I felt like I was waking from a very long sleep. And I felt something else, something small, hard and warm against the back of my middle finger. I opened my eyes.

"She's gone," Agnes said.

I felt drowsy, but happy, like when you wake after a really good dream. There was only Agnes and I standing under the yew tree. I looked around. "And the snow is melting," I said.

I took a half-step back and heard a small gasp escape from Agnes's lips. "Look!" she said, "Oh, look!" She held up her hand. A ray of sun flashed from the gold ring on her finger. "I got it back!" she said. "My mother's wedding ring. I got it back!"

I nodded like I understood. Somehow I had helped Agatha with time travel, but time itself was still a mystery. "That's great." I really meant it.

I moved away from the yew tree. The fire was still burning brightly. Robbie and Will were standing faithfully outside the gap in the hedge.

Will leaned down to look through. "Has she gone?" he called.

"Yes," Agnes and I both called back. "She's gone."

They scurried through, and ran across to us, looking about, stunned. I grabbed two bags of sweets and shoved them in their hands, as though that would make everything normal.

And I looked back at the tree, just to make sure. I couldn't really believe it myself. Water was dripping from the branches. It was like the yew tree was watching the turning of time, and crying.

31

Three nights later, on Christmas Eve, me, Mum, Dad, Esme and Ellie were all together in the living room. The Christmas tree lights were flashing on and off and the twins kept trying to reach out to them. Under the tree were a few Christmas presents. Dad had his big Christmas book out and he read to the twins in his Santa Claus voice, just like he'd read to me when I was little.

Twas the night before Christmas
And all through the house
Not a creature was stirring
Not even a mouse...

Then, when Dad finished his story it was my turn. "Remember Randolph, Mum?"

"Uh-huh. The one Dad said was really a girl?"

I nodded. Dad sunk back into the sofa with his arm round Mum. The twins were asleep on the sheepskin rug. Mum sipped her glass of red wine. "And? What about him? Or her?"

"Well, remember when I was grounded, and you sent me out to buy Jaffa Cakes?"

"And you were away for ages. And it started snowing. Yes, I remember."

"Something tells me," said Dad, "that the Scottish Borders Young Historian of the Year has got a really good story up his sleeve."

I coughed, then carried on. "Well, the thing is, this girl almost got knocked down by a car. It screeched. She screamed. I swung round. She stumbled across the road, tripped over the kerb and grabbed me."

This, I swore, was going to be my last ever lie – and this one was white coloured. Time travel was too weird, and it seemed like there were some things that kids could believe in and adults just couldn't. So I told them the story of Agatha Black, with changes. "Well, she was lost, you know," I told them. "And after she nearly got hit by that car it made her go a bit funny, a bit freaked out. So we hung out for a few days, her and me. I thought it would be easier if we pretended she was a boy. Anyway, I helped her a bit with things. And she helped me. It was fun, actually. She knew loads about history, and she taught me to play chess. I would never have won the history competition without her. Anyway, she's back with her dad now. But she needed some help with the journey home. They don't have any money. I knew it was important, and she was a really good friend, so I… um… I helped her out."

When I came to the end of my story, it dawned on them that there was nothing left of my winnings, and I saw their faces fall. Ever since the prize ceremony, Mum had been suggesting I open a bank account. I'd been shrugging it off. Dad had been telling me to keep my money for the sales, then I could go on a spending spree.

"You gave it *all* away?" Mum shook her head in disbelief. I nodded.

"All of it?" Dad said, and I told them about the twenty-pounds worth of sweets and crisps.

"I can't believe it," Mum said, finishing her wine. She looked at me and shook her head. "You know something, Saul?" I shook my head, wondering what was coming next. "You didn't need to pretend she was a boy."

Dad put his hand on my shoulder. "Your mum's right. But you know what, son? I'm proud of you. If we can't help other folk then we're not worth much." And he hugged me, and so did Mum. And I went off to my room that Christmas Eve the happiest boy in Scotland.

But I couldn't sleep, not right away. I peered out of the window. Most of the snow had disappeared. Just a few white patches were left, lit up in the moonlight, and a shrunken snowman. I pressed my nose against the window and stared out at that tiny snowman for ages, remembering Agatha Black running around the garden laughing, rolling her head, as if it was the best fun ever. And I wondered what she was doing on Christmas Eve, 1812. I hoped, whatever it was, she was laughing, and clapping her hands, and having a right merry time.

In the morning the church bells pealed out Christmas carols. Mum rang a bell through the house and shouted, "Merry Christmas, ho-ho-ho!" and Dad came into my room dressed up in his Santa costume.

The first thing I opened was my stocking at the end of my bed. Inside was a tangerine, an apple, a chocolate golden coin and a torch. I ate the tangerine slowly, imagining it was the most delicious thing in the whole world.

Then I bounded through to the living room, gave Ellie and Esme a kiss for their very first Christmas, then set about opening my presents. I tried to look really surprised at the DVDs, unwrapping them and grinning. I gave Mum and Dad a drawing of our house, which they said was brilliant. Then I tore the paper off socks, books, slippers, selection boxes and a £20 top-up voucher for my phone. Mum was shaking rattles and teddies in front of the twins.

Then Dad disappeared. I heard the front door click open. I heard him wheel something in. My heart thudded. "Merry Christmas, Saul!" he shouted, nudging open the living room door with the front wheel and pushing a green BMX right up to me. "It's not the top of the range, son," he said. "Not even brand new to be honest, but I fixed it up. It's a fine bike, and we hope you like it."

I whooped, jumped up, hugged Mum and Dad and took the handlebars of my very own BMX. It wasn't the one I'd imagined in my magazine. It wasn't like Robbie's. But I didn't care. It looked great. And it was mine.

"Majestic!" I yelled.

3**2**

Visiting the graveyard was Agnes's idea. She'd kept going on about it, about how she'd discovered on a map the exact location of this old graveyard, outside Peebles, and how she was pretty sure Agatha Black would be buried there. I didn't like thinking about Agatha Black being dead. It didn't feel right. So I kept putting Agnes off, suggesting other things to do instead, like teaching me and Robbie and Will to catch fish with our hands. Agnes called it guddling and we got pretty good at it.

It was 1st March, 2013, and the days were getting longer. It was still cold but you could smell spring in the air. I'd even seen a few daffodils. Agnes had taken on Agatha's thing of decorating the den. She had a few flowers dotted about the place because me, Will and Robbie said she could, but she wasn't to overdo it. Sometimes she did overdo it but we didn't really mind. We had all decorated the walls with the few drawings that Agatha had left behind, even although they were kind of strange: pylons, light bulbs, popcorn and street lights. The drawing of me had gone. Now when I go into Mrs Singh's shop I imagine me on the wall, next to the tins of soup!

Mostly our gang played all our games like we'd always done, and forgot that Agnes was a girl, or, well, we knew she was a girl but it was no big deal. She joined in with everything. The best was when she showed us how to climb the tree.

Her dad still played his fiddle on Peebles High Street and Agnes said people really liked hearing music on the street. It cheered them up.

Anyway, this Saturday, 1st March, it was just me and Agnes, and we were playing chess in the den. She was wearing a pair of jeans she'd found in a charity shop and she was looking pretty cool. "If I win," she said, whipping my queen off the board, "I get to choose what we do next."

"Ok," I said, thinking it would be fishing or tree climbing or rabbit catching. Agnes liked stuff like that.

"Check mate," she said, snatching my poor king away. "Graveyard!" she announced, scooping all the chess pieces into the biscuit tin.

I was going to protest when she butted in. "You said ok. Come on, Gang Chief. You can't go back on your word. Don't you want to know what happened?"

I shrugged. That was just the problem. If it was something bad, I didn't want to know. What if Agatha Black had gone back to 1812, caught the measles and died? Or what if she got hung because they said she was a witch? Or what if Dick sold her to the body snatchers? Or what if she never did get back? When I thought about all the "what ifs?" I got a sore head.

Agnes pulled at my sleeve. "Come on, Saul. It'll be an adventure." Then she ran out of the den, grabbed her bike (Robbie had given her his old one after he got a newer model) and squirmed through the gap in the hedge.

I followed her, steering my BMX out and over the wasteland. We started pedalling as soon as we reached a road, racing each other out to the edge of Peebles. The old graveyard was in the country near Neidpath Castle, not the one I walk through to get to school. Agnes said her grandmother often went to this country one, with flowers.

We wound up a narrow lane, going further up and up into the hills. My bike was great. I didn't care that it wasn't the most expensive kind. Since meeting Agatha Black I'd learnt a lot of things. Loving my second-hand bike was one of them.

I slowed down as a stone wall came into view behind a clump of fir trees. What else, I wondered – my heart pounding hard and not only because of the cycling – was I going to learn? "I think we should leave our bikes here," I said, propping mine against the stone wall.

Agnes did the same, her face all pink and shiny. She smiled at me, nervously I thought, the way she chewed her bottom lip. "You ready for this, Saul?"

I nodded, but the truth was I wasn't. I wanted to remember Agatha alive, the way she was just before Christmas. I wanted to remember her laughing and making fire and telling her stories and being so sad for Bob Cratchet. It didn't seem right that we were going to try and find her grave.

The old graveyard, next to Neidpath Castle, is one of the creepiest places in Peebles. We walked around the outside, looking for a gate. Near us, mountain-bikers whizzed by on rough tracks, throwing up mud and panting hard. This hill was famous for bike trails. The bikers zooming past weren't thinking about the ancient skeletons close by.

Agnes and I didn't say a word but padded on over the mossy ground. We found a rusty high gate, but it was locked. An old sign on the gate said

OPEN SUNDAYS 2–3PM

Agnes hoisted herself up and clambered over. I followed her, wobbling on a rusty bar and struggling to get my leg over the top. Then I had to jump about ten feet down. I landed in springy moss and rolled over. Sitting in the thick grass I swallowed hard. We were in the ancient graveyard.

Agnes was already peering at a gravestone. "Wilemina Baxter," she read, "died 1871, aged 17."

I got up and looked around. There were loads of gravestones. Some were stone angels with broken wings. Some were simple crosses. Others were slabs in the ground, mossed over. I staggered backwards, realising I was standing on one.

"Poor Wilemina," Agnes said, "I wonder what she died of?" She moved on. "This one – Helen – died aged two! Probably consumption."

I cast my eyes around the old cemetery, and shivered. It would take forever to examine every stone. A blackbird landed on a gravestone in front of me. It sang and flew off. I watched it go, swooping up and down and disappearing into the dark green branches of a tree. "There's a yew tree," I said. "Look! Over there!" The branches of the tree hung over mossy graves. "Maybe she's under there," I said, pulling Agnes away from wee Helen. I felt a prickle up the back of my neck. "But I don't know if I want to know."

"We've come this far," Agnes said, "we might as well know. Come on, and you're probably right. It would be like Agatha to ask to be buried under a yew tree."

We walked over. The sun threw gravestone shadows on the grass. The bird had stopped singing and it felt so quiet in there, you could almost hear the dead whisper.

I thought of Agatha screaming, running over the road and grabbing my ankles. I remembered a snowflake falling and landing on her long black eyelashes, and how she smiled so her pale blue eyes sparkled. I remembered the way she said "Majestic!" And how she taught me to play chess, and how she let me cut her hair and how she said she wanted to be called Randolph, and how she said she was good and true. And how she slept all by herself in the den and how she laughed when I suggested eating oranges. And how she said she would never forget me. Ever.

"It's all mossed over," Agnes said, tugging my arm. I blinked. I looked down. We had reached the yew tree and right under it stood an old gravestone. A bunch of faded meadow flowers lay on the ground next to it. Was this *the* gravestone? I shuddered. The yew branches made a shushing sound in the wind.

I sunk to my knees and pulled the moss away. It fell

off in my hands showing the writing carved into the stone underneath. "That's it!" Agnes cried. "Oh! It is! It's hers!"

She fell to her knees beside me. In a trembling voice she read out the inscription:

AGATHA FORSYTH, NÉE BLACK

BORN 21ST JUNE, 1802
DIED 31ST DECEMBER, 1879

DEARLY BELOVED WIFE OF
HECTOR FORSYTH, SCHOOLMASTER
MUCH-LOVED MOTHER OF
AGNES & SAUL

Agnes gasped. I watched her fumble in a bag she'd brought. Then she scooped up a handful of soft earth and planted a primrose beside the grave. In the tree above us the blackbird started singing again. With a lump in my throat I read out the very last words, carved in stone at the bottom:

ALIVE IN OUR HEARTS FOREVER

AFTERWORD

The character of Agatha Black is inspired by a real girl: Marjory Fleming. Marjory was born on the 15th January, 1803 in Kirkcaldy, Fife, Scotland. At the tender age of six she went off to Edinburgh town where she had lessons from her beloved and very patient cousin, Isabella Keith. To help with her writing, Isabella suggested that the young "all thunderstorms and sunshine" Marjory keep a journal. Between 1810 and 1811, aged seven and eight, Marjory filled three slim notebooks with her own individual observations and poems, covering subjects as varied as literature, love, history and religion.

Marjory Fleming's aunt had a pet monkey called Pug who lived with them in the house in Charlotte Square, Edinburgh. He was clearly a popular attraction and Marjory wrote of him, "the monkey gets as many visitors as I or my cousins."

After returning to Kirkcaldy, Marjory wrote in a letter to Isabella, on 1st September 1811, "we are surrounded by the measles on every side." On 19th December 1811 Marjory died, shortly before her ninth birthday.

Half a century later, Mark Twain, on reading her letters, journals and poems, referred to her as a "wonder child."

Marjory Fleming is buried in Abbotshall Churchyard in Kirkcaldy. The original and very modest gravestone, simply inscribed "M F 1811", can still be seen. Next to the gravestone is a statue of a young girl writing, erected in 1930, dedicated to her as the "Youngest Immortal".

Marjory Fleming's original diaries are kept in the National Library of Scotland. I am indebted to a beautiful published volume, *Marjory's Book: The complete journals, letters and poems of a young girl,* edited by Barbara Mclean (Mercat Press).

Janis Mackay
Edinburgh, December 2012